First

New writing by young people
from the north of England

New Writing North

First published in Great Britain by New Writing North 2003
Copyright © individual authors
The moral rights of all of the authors have been asserted
New Writing North, 7-8 Trinity Chare, Quayside, Newcastle upon Tyne, NE1 3DF
ISBN 0-9541456-1-5
Printed on Tyneside by Peterson Printers

Introduction

New Writing North, as the writing development agency for the north of England, works with writers and aspiring writers at all stages of their careers. In 1999, thanks to the Regional Arts Lottery Programme, we were able to launch a new three-year project, Juice.

The Juice project was created to facilitate new ways for young people, both in school and outside of school, to get involved with creative writing. The project encompassed a range of activity, from writers' residencies in schools to free creative writing classes for young people over 16 in Sunderland, Middlesbrough, Whitehaven and Newcastle upon Tyne. Once we began the creative writing classes we began to realise just how much young writing talent there was in the region.

In 2002 we launched the first Northern Young Writer's Competition so that a wider group of writers would have the chance to submit their work for publication. The work in this book reflects the very best work from the competition and comes from young writers from across the region - from Hartlepool to Barrow in Furness.

One of the writers in this book will go on to be awarded the title of Northern Young Writer of the Year at this year's Northern Writers' Awards ceremony, where they will also receive a cash prize. We also hope to be able to help the most promising writers from this book to develop their work further in the future.

The work in this book reflects a wide range of inspirations and themes. We were delighted to receive both well written and original work from so many contributors. The stories look both to the past and to the future, but many take place very much here and now, reflecting real experiences, situations and emotions.

We wish all of the contributors well with their future writing projects and look forward to seeing more of their work in print in the future.

Acknowledgments

This book, like so many of New Writing North's projects, would not have been made possible were it not for the support of a number of the north east's most talented writers.

Novelist Andrea Badenoch and the poets Cynthia Fuller and Gordon Hodgeon sifted entries to the competition and worked with all the contributors editorially on their submissions prior to publication. I thank them all for their expert help.

Writing classes for young writers were tutored by Carina Rodney, Barrie Darke, Paul Summers, Ian Dowson and Subhadassi. Visiting writers who gave of their time to visit the groups included Chrissie Glazebrook, Claire Pollard and Laura Hird.

Thanks also to John Adair for copy editing and page design, to Dan and Jim at Sumo for the cover design and to John McGagh for administrative support with the project.

The Juice project was made possible by financial support from the Regional Arts Lottery Programme, Northern Arts, the Esmee Fairbairn Foundation, the Sponsors Club, The Community Foundation North East (via the Newcastle Building Society Community Fund), Whitehaven Council, Middlesbrough Borough Council, Sunderland Arts and Libraries and Durham County Council Local Education Authority.

Claire Malcolm
Director, New Writing North, February 2003

Contents

Upside Dream	7	Graeme Beech
Bored and blacked out	8	Graeme Beech
Jay's Room	9	AJ Barron
Disconnected	18	Robert Steggles
Elna's War	20	Beth Timson
The Deal	28	Karen Hands
Rocks of Utah	31	Katherine Eyre
Station	32	Katherine Eyre
Leeds	33	Leo Wilkinson
Bush being told - 11th September	36	Joanne Shields
Too Far	38	Joanne Shields
The Mistake	39	Charlie Keys
The Beginning of the End	42	Emily Hudson
Be aware of how we work	45	Roxie Willows
African Story	46	Hannah Glancy
A Different Time	50	Jodie Gray
The One who Destroys	52	Stephanie Fisher
We Have Rights	53	Stephanie Fisher
Down Comes Rain	54	Helen Fairgrieve
Bounce	57	Dave Rinaldi and Briony Chown
Thankyou	58	Dave Rinaldi

Contents

By Blood by Fire	59	Ruth Gilfillan
Tramp	64	Georgina Ascroft
The Hole	68	Penny West
Seascale Pier	78	Tom Fletcher
A Conversation	80	Joanne Shields
A Relationship	87	Rebecca Jones
Ghost	88	Gary Irving
A Split	93	Thom Hurst
Short Toll	93	Thom Hurst
Ghost Girl	94	Lisa Maughan
Spider	104	Peter Morgan
Esther Wood	105	Hope Whitmore
Searching for Silence	110	Helen Koelmans
Drink	112	Neil Singh
The Comfort of Fear	113	Dominic Freeston
Love, Sex and Cider	118	Paul Charlton
Bumblebee	129	Ellie Slee
Memory Woman	130	Emma McGordon
Heat	132	Emma McGordon
When Hitler was my Daddy	133	Emma McGordon

Upside dream

I am in the shadow
Of the speck
On the distant lit up ceiling
And small as I can know.

And on that barren land of ceiling
I am dreaming
About the world,
And about the strings of dancing dust
That are trembling just for me.

I am in the shadow
Of the speck
On the distant lit up ceiling
And this is all I know.

Graeme Beech

Bored and Blacked Out

As I lick the dry wax ribbed
Cathedral roofing of my mouth
My tongue goes fuzzy numb.
Lets up, limp, exhausted,
And dies upon the floor.

Later an orb of water pushes outward
Pulsing through my skull
Once a minute or so,
A concentrated clock.

Slipping on my seat
I am reminded by my eyes,
And I do not want to be reminded
Of this or my crimson filled head,
Or that I am just alive.
I am bored and blacking out
And I hope that he can hear.

Graeme Beech

GRAEME BEECH is 19 and lives in Sunderland. He started to write poetry when he was 16 and his poem is inspired by "my realisation that looking upon solitude, either literally or spiritually, reveals an obscure and foul beauty that can only be seized in writing". He hopes to write professionally in the future.

Jay's Room

AJ Barron

A few seconds after I knocked, Jay's voice floated through the frosted glass of the front door and told me it was open. I found myself on the landing, looking up the staircase of the house he was no longer welcome in.

That morning I had been woken by a phone call from Jay asking me if I would help him move all of his belongings from his current home and pack them into the van that he had hired to take him to his new flat on a nearby estate.

I agreed and he told me what time to come round.

As I followed the stairs up to the top I saw Jay's head lean over the banister, his hair falling to one side.

"Alright," he said.

I said the same in return.

Before climbing the stairs I'd looked into the open doorway of the living room, where I could see that he had already moved some of the boxes from upstairs. His bedroom was a loft conversion which had added an extra storey to the house.

The last time I'd seen Jay was a few days beforehand. I had a job in a town centre bar during the summer and would often work long day-shifts during which the place would remain almost empty, busy moments only coming from a handful of consumers wanting to get out of the sun or a flock of shop assistants after closing time.

The majority of my shifts were spent sitting on a bar stool by the large window through which the midday sun was amplified, sometimes stealing a cold bottle of lager when the manager wasn't around.

It was during one of these hot days that I saw Jay walk past the window wearing his usual biker boots and long black trench coat, his greasy blond hair bouncing over its wide collar. Knowing I worked there, I thought he may look in my direction. He did.

I waved.

He waved back and headed towards the entrance. I returned to the bar.

After saying our hellos and shaking hands, I asked what he had been up to. It had been a few months since I'd seen him last.

Ordering a pint of Guinness first, he said: "I've just been to the doctors to try and convince him that I'm depressed... I was hoping he might put me on Prozac."

"Why?" I asked.

"The council might give me a flat quicker if I'm clinically depressed." He smiled.

I began to realise that a lot must have happened since the last time we'd met.

"I've been wandering the streets for the last three weeks," he continued. "My mam's kicked me out."

"Why?"

Jay just shrugged.

It had always been a strange relationship as both Jay and his mother tended to drink heavily. They would often argue, he told me, but I never asked what about.

The only real reason I could think of, although I didn't want to say, why Jay may have been asked to return his key, was on account of his girlfriend, Linda. Jay had met her where they both worked at the local Halfords. Jay was 18. Linda was 33 and had two young sons. There were two main people who opposed the relationship: Jay's mother and Linda's husband, who she had left for Jay.

The husband would visit Linda's house when Jay was there and say: "Shouldn't you be at school, son?"

"He's a fat ugly bastard!" Jay would say whenever telling me the latest insult the husband had thrown at him.

He'd told me about her a few times before they'd got together. About the flirtation on the shop floor and the first time he'd taken Linda to his house to meet his mother and the argument that followed.

"It's probably that whole situation that's pissed Mam off so much," he told me as he downed a quarter of his pint. "She doesn't want the hassle, and she doesn't like Linda, so she wants me gone."

Jay went on to tell me about the last three weeks. He'd spent the time bouncing around from house to house; his friend Peter's and Linda's, and spending his days on the streets when he wasn't at work. He'd spent one night in a church doorway behind the high street, hoping that it would help him get a house sooner. It hadn't. He'd never called me to ask if he could stay at mine. The depression idea was his latest. "But the doctor would only prescribe Paracetemol," he said. "If I was pregnant I'd have a house straight away."

Jay was silent for a while.

"She's taken everything away from me," he said as he rolled a cigarette, sighing, speaking in the melodramatic way he always did. "My mam has, you know what I mean?"

"Yeah," I said.

After I was up to speed on his story and a few more pints later, Jay left the bar to circle the town a few more times before Linda finished work. He told me he'd ring me in the next couple of days or when he got a flat. I said okay, knowing that I probably wouldn't see him again for months.

But it was only two days later when Jay called and told me that he'd been granted a flat and needed help moving his stuff.

Jay hadn't gone into much detail over the phone. All he said was that the new flat had one bedroom and was about two miles away from his mother's. Today we had the house to ourselves so there was no chance of an uncomfortable run-in as she was taking a week's holiday, spending the money she had saved for Jay's university tuition. Jay was no longer going to college; instead he was trying to get a full-time position at Halfords. It would be one more thing that separated me and him as I would be going away to university in a few months.

Jay didn't think about it too much anymore. He was just eager to remove his stuff while his mother was gone in order to lessen the chances of her finding out where he was moving to. Then he could start again from scratch.

"There's a lot more stuff to come down yet," he told me, indicating towards upstairs.

"No problem," I said. "Be alright with the two of us."

He thanked me for coming.

"It's OK."

When we reached the top of the fragile staircase that led to his loft room I found that it had changed completely from the last time I'd seen it. The Jay's room I had known had been covered by band posters, band names constructed with white tape across the varnished beams that held up the slanted ceiling. That leaning wall gave the room a triangular look, and on it was a window that opened outwards. The glass gave way to an amazing view of the sea which lay over the tiled roofs which stretched out to the beach and revealed the two lighthouses in the distance. Miles apart, piers wrapped round the water and sand like hugging arms. On a day as clear and sunny as this one you could see everything from that window; the beach, the fairground and a quarter of the basketball courts. The sun illuminated the constant flux of surf which poured steadily in. It was a perfectly balanced sight, being able to view the nothingness on the horizon whilst still surrounded by claustrophobic suburbia.

The view was the only aspect of Jay's room that had remained the same.

Everything else had been altered by his mother. She'd taken down his posters and stripped the walls bare of the paper underneath, leaving them grey and the beams free of sticky tape.

All that was left was a number of boxes of various sizes and weights, an empty chest of drawers, a desk and a neatly made bed, still with quilt cover and sheets.

"Are you taking the bed?" I asked.

"No," Jay smiled. "I've been told that it stays."

"What are you supposed to use then?"

"I've got a mattress," he said, pointing to where it lay folded up in the corner, beaten and spitting sponge. "Anyway, that's the least of my worries," he continued, telling me that the new place had no hot water, carpets, cooker or fridge. Even the doors of the kitchen cupboards had been stolen by the previous tenant. And now he had only a mattress to sleep on.

In Jay's eyes there was something that made up for all of this though. Despite the lack of belongings this was still going to be Jay's place, and Jay's place alone. That was all he needed.

"I've definitely got more stuff than I told the removal men I had," he told me. "I had to tell them everything I wanted to take over on the phone. I had to list it all, but there's more than I thought. He looked worried. "Hope he doesn't charge over thirty quid, cos that's all I've got."

"So we're taking everything but the bed?" I said.

"Yeah. Everything goes."

Jay decided it would be better if we moved all the heavier items downstairs first. We took the desk, tipping it to one side and manoeuvring it long-ways down the two narrow staircases, scraping the wallpaper as we went.

"I don't give a shit if we damage the walls," said Jay.

Next came the large armchair, the only real piece of furniture he was allowed to take with him. We almost ripped the banister off with it before finding a successful way of carrying it down.

Boxes and other minor items of furniture soon accumulated in the living room and began blocking the doorway. As the living room filled the bedroom emptied until all the boxes were gone from it, leaving only the bed with its neat sheets and quilt.

"I was thinking of writing something on the wall before I left," Jay said. "Something like 'Farewell cruel world'."

I secretly grimaced at the suggestion.

One of the beams which stretched horizontally across the ceiling had a short wooden pole attached to it by two metal rods. It was for coat hangers and belts. Taking a screwdriver from his toolkit, Jay decided to remove it, telling me that he could use it in the wardrobe of his new flat as it had no hanger rail.

Jay wanted to take everything he could.

We began laughing about it as we added the pole, rods and screws to the pile in the living room.

We were hot and sweating as we stood back and saw that everything that was to be taken had been. There was nothing left in Jay's room for us. And yet, after we both had a glass of room temperature tap water we went back upstairs to take one last look.

I could understand why Jay would want to do that – this had been his home for a long time. But why I decided to go back up there with him, I can't tell. The space had no emotional significance for me. But still I followed.

It was intense for a while as Jay and I just stood there, looking around; neither of us speaking. I began to feel the urge to talk, say anything to relieve the tension.

"You should take the carpet," I said.

Jay laughed.

It was a rough green carpet, blemished by stamped-in chewing gum and cigarette burns. It wasn't attached to the floor, I noticed. Not even at the corners.

The thought of removing the carpet soon stopped being a joke.

"Let's take the carpet!" I insisted.

Jay sucked noisily through his teeth. "Eh?"

"Why not? You said you haven't got any carpets," I said, looking around the floor. "This'll probably fill out your sitting room easily."

Laughing it off, Jay said: "She'd go berserk."

"And? She's thrown you out. Fuck her!"

I wanted Jay to take the carpet. I felt as if I'd scream at him if he didn't. I was so wrapped up in the idea I couldn't tell whether I actually thought it would be good for his new place or if I was just making trouble. It made me happy to think of how angry his mother would be when she found out. He needed to get one over on her before he was gone. This was a woman who had called him at Linda's house asking him to pay the board money he owed for the three weeks he had been homeless. I had only met Jay's mother a few times and so felt like the devil sitting on his shoulder, my lack of inclusion in the situation making me free to incite recklessness.

"OK," said Jay.

Our only problem with removing the carpet was the neatly made bed still in the centre of the room. Lifting it from the boards we rolled it up tightly to the bottom legs of the bed, lifted that end and rolled it underneath. We then did the same at the other end. Getting it down the stairs on our shoulders ended in me banging my shin against the banister.

"I wonder if I should take the stereo as well," Jay said as I leaned over rubbing the dead skin from the graze. He was looking at the small CD player on the coffee table at the other end of the room. "That was mine before I got the new one. I should take it just to piss her off."

I looked at the stereo, then at Jay.

"Take it."

"OK."

Unplugging the stereo, Jay added it to the pile.

We couldn't call it Jay's room anymore. Everything was gone, the room echoing because of our now noticeable footsteps as we went back in.

Jay took a tobacco tin with a faded picture of Kurt Cobain on it from his pocket and a packet of Rizlas. Sitting on the bare floorboards, dust collecting on our trousers, I watched as he expertly crafted a cigarette. I said nothing as he rolled so as not to break the intense look of concentration on his face.

"You want one?" he asked without even looking at me, rolling his tongue along the edge of the paper and sticking it down, completing the faultless cylinder.

"Yeah," I said, even though I didn't smoke.

He passed me the roll-up he'd just made and began on another. Before putting it in my mouth, I first inspected it, impressed by Jay's craftsmanship. It was a skill he'd acquired over about two years of buying tobacco by the pouch instead of by the packet. "It works out much cheaper," he explained.

I lit it and puffed heavily, feeling every toxin and tar particle as it hit my lungs. It was harsh, without a filter, and I tried not to cough.

Standing up I opened he window, taking a good look at the view for what would probably be the last time.

"I'm gonna miss that view," said Jay from the floor, lighting his cigarette. I allowed mine to burn out in the ashtray by his knee.

"Let's take that as well," I said.

"What?" said Jay, smoke flowing through his nostrils.

"The view! We should take that too."

Jay grinned. "She'd go nuts it I took that."

"She doesn't know where you live."

So Jay and I leaned out of the window as far as we could, our chests touching the cold chipped slates of the roof, and began tugging the view away from its seams. It made a ripping sound that echoed throughout the estate as it came jaggedly away from the sky like torn fabric. Once we'd dragged it through the window completely we evened it out on the floorboards, the sea breeze still coming from inside it, blowing our hair, the sound of gulls and kids' voices still clearly audible. The sunlight which it still held filled the room as if we were outside.

"Careful you don't fall in," said Jay as it covered the entire floor, forcing us on tiptoe against the skirting boards.

Looking down into the view I could still make out the sea clearly as a cruise ship came out between the piers and headed out. I put my hand into it, feeling the close air, the heat from the sun. Jay tried to catch a large fly as it flew into the room from the view and zig-zagged along the walls.

Taking each end carefully, Jay and I walked towards each other, folding the view like a sheet, cutting off some of the sounds and the breeze, the natural light of his bedroom returning to normal. We folded it again and again until eventually it was small enough to fit in the leg pocket of Jay's combat trousers. Holding it up to my ear before it was put away I could hear the sounds of traffic on the coast road and a dog barking in the distance.

Jay closed the window. There was nothing to see anymore.

"That'll be helpful," he said. "The only thing outside the window in my place is a knackered wooden fence." He laughed. Looking along the ceiling and the sloping wall, he said, "I bet I could use those beams for bookshelves."

"The floorboards could be useful too," I suggested.

Carefully we pulled those up as well, snapping one in two by accident as we carried it down the stairs.

Without saying anything we had decided that it was Jay's right to take everything. Everything but the bed.

Continuing with the hammer and screwdriver we knocked the plaster from the walls and then chipped away the concrete from around the bricks underneath, collecting it all into the plastic carrier bags that Jay's mother kept under the kitchen sink. We took the bricks from the wall and transported them all downstairs by the armful, scraping our skin. The window, still attached to the window frame, was removed; the ceiling and roof tiles above that went also. With an envelope and dustpan and brush we carefully collected all of the dust from around the skirting boards, trying not to breathe too heavily as we did so. Finally, we took the heavy support beams from beneath the floorboards.

By now it was impossible to move around in the living room anymore as it was so cluttered by furniture and architecture that the debris began spilling onto the landing.

All that was left of Jay's room was a spacious void without even a skyline surrounding it, populated by nothing but a neatly made bed.

The loud knock at the front door told us that the removal men had arrived, 25 minutes late. Jay and I were sitting on the stairway, the only free space left, still breathing heavily and bathed in sweat. We looked at the clutter around us, our exhaustion increasing as we realised we were going to have to do the whole thing over again.

Jay carefully navigated his way through his deconstructed room to the doorway. The sunshine illuminated the staircase as he opened the door.

There was some swift conversation before Jay allowed the two men in. I noticed that one of them was missing an eye. It was nothing but the upper lid pulled over the lower. His functioning eye was menacing enough as he glared at me through the pale blueness of his pupil, catching me looking at his deformity. The other stood silently in the background, looking at what had accumulated in the living room.

"What wuh takin thun?" asked one eye.

Jay waved his hand over the clutter and said: "Everything in here: all the boxes, the desk, the chair, the mattress, the bookcase, the chest of drawers, the beams, the floorboards, the bricks, the bags of broken plaster, the windows, the envelope of dust over there and the view from my bedroom window, but I've got that in my pocket." He patted the leg of his combats.

I expected the removal men to quote Jay a new price because of the increased amount he now wanted to take. More than he could afford.

"Reet thun," said one eye, rubbing his rough palms together. "Let's git started."

From outside, the red removal van looked small, but after the agonising fifteen minutes of hefting Jay's room from A to B we realised that a lot more could have comfortably fitted in there. It was only a quarter full.

With everything packed in and secured, I rode to Jay's new flat in the back of the van along with the removal man who had both of his eyes. He was small and fat, curly black hair escaping from underneath his cap. He kept staring at me the whole time we were travelling.

The idea of the one-eyed man driving made me nervous.

It was a difficult journey because there was no way we could see where we were going. I was thrown from side to side each time we took a corner.

I held onto the sharp rails on the walls of the van as the mattress slid from Jay's armchair and took my legs from under me.

The removal man looked at me through his two eyes and smiled each time I lost balance. He could take the journey without holding on or stumbling, he'd done it so often.

"Doesn't look big, the van," he said, "but ye can fit plenty in."

I nodded and smiled.

"Yeah, ye could fit a three bedroom house inside here," he told me proudly looking the inside of the van up and down.

A J BARRON is 21 and lives in South Shields. He is inspired by the writers Yukio Mishima, Haruki Murakami, Charles Bukowski and William Burroughs. He hopes to write full time in the future.

Disconnected

You looked over
Now it had ended
You couldn't speak
It was a mess

Thick black smoke drifted from the engine
The dull green bonnet lay still now
Twisted and broken
I couldn't hear any thing
You spoke
But your words meant nothing any more

The window shield was smashed
It dripped with our blood
Separated
Your blood to the right
My blood to the left

As I stared at you I could feel the blood running slowly down my face
It ran into my mouth
I could taste the bitterness

The sirens began
The blue lights swayed against the dented tree
Now broken

I watched as you turned around
Only now to notice that she lay there
Twisted and shattered
You gripped your bottle tighter
Your hands soaked with blood

You slowly turned around
Facing the wreck that lay ahead of you
And let out an angry scream
You closed your eyes tightly
Because now you know we were all
Disconnected

Robert Steggles

ROBERT STEGGLES is 16 and lives in County Durham. He started writing at the age of 12 and is inspired by books, television, music and people. His poem is influenced by the "constant stories on TV and in newspapers about careless people who drink and drive".

Elna's War

Beth Timson

The soldiers poured over the hillsides around the village during the night. They weren't silent, the scramble of boots on the rocky paths and whispered orders as groups of men were put into position echoed off the terrain. Below, in the valley, however, nobody was woken, the farmers, their wives and their children slept soundly.

Just up the left hand path from the north end of the village there was a little stream tumbling down to meet the Ninle river. Near its source, Pablo bent his head to drink the icy water. He had been fighting in this silent war for six months now but like so many others had seen no real action. As the army had slowly crept north from the provinces, attracting very little attention (uprisings of this sort were common) it had swallowed village after village, advancing on the capital. In the days to come they would make the final push and he was here helping hold the valley – they needed it, as the major route in Caruna ran through it.

Climbing up the steep banks that the stream had carved into the rock he returned to his unit and lit a cigarette. In the darkness it glowed orange and he sat with the other staring at the mountains in the distance, waiting.

In the village of Nine, within the small house behind the bakery, a young boy drifted feverishly in and out of sleep. His bed covers were twisted round his legs and the sweat poured from his face. In the next room the baker and his wife debated, in whispers what to do with their child, trying not to wake the others. Three more boys and two girls lay on mattresses around them, while the baby slept in a box in the corner. Mother couldn't leave the children and father couldn't leave his work, they needed the money. The eldest, a girl called Elna, would have to take the three-year-old to the hospital in Caruna; they would wake her at dawn.

The old baker pushed the few coins he had into Elna's hand and urged her to put them into the bag around her waist with the food. "It should only take you a day or so to get there but as long as they keep him in, you stay. Don't go off into the city alone."

"Don't worry," she tried to smile reassuringly as her mother handed her the boy. He weighed hardly anything but it would be awkward to get him through the mountains. With kisses form her parents, Elna finally shuffled out of the door and began to walk up the valley. By midday she was four miles away and starting to tire so, carefully laying her brother down beside her, she stopped to rest and took some bread out of her bag to feed him. He refused to take it so she poured some water into his mouth and ate it herself. Ahead of them was the pass through the mountains, an easy enough road but they wouldn't make it through by nightfall so she'd have to find somewhere to sleep. After a while the aching in her arms began to ease a little so she picked everything up and set off again.

Elna woke the next morning as the first drops of rain fell. Gathering everything she hoisted the toddler onto her hip and felt his temperature. The fever had shown signs of relenting when they settled down but a night out in the cold had made him worse than ever. It was a good job she could see down the road into Caruna and she hurried the last half a mile, arriving just as the city was stirring awake. As the shutters went up to open one of the shops, she tapped on the window and beckoned the boy inside to come and talk to her. He opened the door and looked her up and down warily.

"What do you want?"

"Please could you tell me the way to the hospital?"

"Why do you want to go there?" Standing on the step above her he looked down his nose at the girl and suddenly noticed the bundle she was carrying move.

"You got a kid there?"

"He's my brother, I need to get him to the hospital." She was growing impatient.

"Suppose I'll help you then. Come on. I'll show you the way."

"You don't have to come..."

"Nah, I couldn't describe it to you, I don't know the difference between left and right."

They both laughed.

Tugging her hand he led her down an alley between two houses and they came out onto a road full of people setting off for work. Just along the street he stopped and pointed upwards at the red cross sign. She thanked him before he left. As she stepped inside, the first claps of thunder sounded. She suddenly realised how tired she was and, having let a strange pair of arms take her brother, Elna let herself be guided to a bed nearby.

She was conscious of the bustle of nurses round her brother as they saw to him and with the knowledge that he would be alright she finally relaxed enough to fall into a proper sleep. Later that day she woke, expecting to be in her own home, but no, she was in the hospital and something was happening, in the dusk outside,

An army jeep rattled to a stop on the road below, allowing two men to jump off the back before continuing down the valley. Puzzled, Pablo leapt from the rock he had been perched on and made his way down the steep hillside. At the bottom he found three men deep in discussion and went over. "Ah, Pablo, you can do it, orders just come through from the general. We have to stop all non-essential traffic along this road so I want you to take any men you can find and set up a checkpoint at the entry to the mountain pass. If anyone asks, you're in charge." Pablo nodded respectfully and set off wondering if this meant that an assault on Caruna was imminent.

Back in Nine the baker wasn't concentrating on his work. He was standing by his shop window, staring out onto the street anxiously. The army was bringing its troops up through the village in preparation for moving into the city. He had seen attempts at this before, the rural north had always felt separated and dictated over by the city and calls for revolution were strong. Yet nothing had ever been produced on this scale before, hundreds of men in organised rank and with real weapons moved along the road, accompanied by wagons full of ammunition.

He was anxious because it would make his daughter's return dangerous so he stood and deliberated whether to go and get the children himself. When an hour later another wave of men passed through he made up his mind to go. Grabbing an old coat he stepped out into the rain and hurried up the road. Not having anything to carry he made much faster progress than Elna had and was nearing the pass when a rough hand held him by the shoulder and pulled him off the road. Pablo shook the old man and told him he couldn't get through.

"But I need to get to my children... please... it's urgent," the baker begged, his face full of desperation. Pablo didn't have time for this; he wanted to persuade someone to relieve him of his post so he could join the fighting. "No, I'm sorry but I can't let anyone through. Now go back or I'll have to force you." And with that he gave the old man a shove back in the direction of the village and went back to stand under the shelter of a tree as he watched him disappear into the rain.

The room shook as a bomb hit a building across the street. Elna sat up and looked across at her sleeping brother before glancing up, worried, at a doctor hurrying down the ward towards her. His white coat was torn and he stopped when he reached them to check the boy.

"He will survive. I am afraid you will have to leave, make sure that he gets rest and proper food."

"But we can't go. He isn't all better yet!"

"I'm sorry but we need the space. I have to get rid of all non-emergencies and he should be all right as long as you look after him so that the fever doesn't take hold again. We've done all we can. He'll be fine as long as you look after him. Now, I'm sorry but please, you have to leave." And with that he gave her the child and began to empty the rest of the ward. Elna was hurried away by a nurse and found herself at the entrance she had come in through less than a day before. This time though the square was in chaos. People were frantically digging through a building that had collapsed, a pipe had burst and the air was full of the sounds of bullets and explosions from other parts of the city. Stepping out onto the pavement she had to clutch her brother as someone ran into her.

"Sorry love, I'd go home if I were you, take cover, it isn't safe here," said the man, out of breath.

"I'm going to..." But he'd hurried on his way and besides Elna didn't know what she was going to do. They couldn't stay on the streets, or anywhere in the city for that matter, but she had to find somewhere she could look after her brother. Maybe I should find someone who'll let us stay for a while in their house, she thought, and with that set off in the opposite direction to most of the noise. This involved going through a new part of Caruna and they were soon lost.

Coming to the end of a street full of official looking offices she found herself in front of a huge, very old building. It was where the country's parliament worked and she'd seen it often in pictures but today it was different. Soldiers were trying to force in the main entrance and some of the workers, who had obviously locked themselves in, were leaning out of windows throwing anything they could find, including abuse, onto the heads below. Elna felt the ground shake as an explosion shattered the majestic, solid doors, and she cowered back into a doorway seeking protection and a place to hide from the hundreds of men now pouring towards the building. Suddenly she was being covered in plaster and rubble as something hit the house behind her and she bent over to protect the toddler in her arms.

After a moment everything settled and she realised that her right arm hurt. The fingers were covered in blood and she could only move the shoulder, the rest of it hung limply by her side. Scrabbling up she managed to drag them to a wall. The house behind them had been completely blown away and she slumped next to a pile of what looked as if it had been the kitchen.

The rain was falling harder than ever so she was drenched and freezing cold as well as full of pain from her arm. Elna began to feel herself drifting into unconsciousness as the pain became too much. Her brother was crying but there was nothing she could do. The glow of the fire burning somewhere in the rubble was fading and she could no longer feel the cold of the rain but then there was something on her shoulder, a hand. From nowhere, someone was lifting her up and the crying had stopped. She ate some of the food she was given and became aware that they were moving. Opening her eyes she felt a little strength come back and peering up into the gathering darkness recognised a familiar face. It was the boy who had shown them the way to the hospital.

"Hello, awake now are you? You're brother's fast asleep."

"Where is he? Where are we going?" Elna tried to lift herself up but as soon as she was vertical fell back against something. Looking around she realised that they were in the back of an old pick-up with what looked like the rest of his family.

"I'm Jan, we're taking you away from the fighting. It's alright – your brother is with my sister."

"Where are we going? The doctor said that he needed rest."

"Into the hills, everyone is leaving the city, our shop was hit – we have nowhere else to go." Elna sat up suddenly in panic.

"I have to get him home, back to Nine. Our parents are there and they will know how to look after him. If we don't find a proper place to stay the fever will come back."

"You can't go back to Nine, the mountain pass is blocked, it's how they're getting all their troops into the city. You'll be killed."

"Where else can we go? He will die if we don't." Elna crawled forward to where Jan's sister was and took her brother.

"I'm sorry but I can't... this isn't the right way." And with that she let the gate at the back of the truck down and slid off onto the road. She'll get herself killed if she goes back through the city and how would she carry the kid with a broken arm? The stupid girl, thought Jan. But what else could he do? She'd blown her chance but then again he couldn't just watch her disappear. With a last, apologetic, glance at his sister, he too slid off the back of the truck and rolled over in the dirt of the road. Elna watched him walk over, her arm was hurting and she was shivering from the cold and wet.

"I need to get him home," she said, almost too tired to talk.

"Don't be an idiot, they'll kill you if you try to get through those mountains."

"I've got to try." He looked at the girl, stubborn and dirty, and almost regretted ever helping her but he was in it now. Picking up the boy, he said, "Well you're stupid but I'm going to help you for his sake because otherwise you'll get the pair of you killed. Understand?" She nodded guiltily.

"Come on then, we can't go through the fighting, we'll have to go round it". So he led them through the darkness.

The slopes of the hillsides around the city were covered in forest and it was among these trees that Pablo now sat watching over the road into Caruna, under orders to shoot anyone who refused to go back into the city. If the army couldn't keep everyone inside for the next day or so they would just be getting in the way of their preparations. They were going to set up a new government, one that would pay attention to the problems of the whole country, not just the city. They needed this road clear so that they could bring in all the people and materials needed to do this.

At the bottom of the road a gate had been set up to stop people getting through, while, like him, many soldiers had been sent to look out for anyone trying to sneak past. Pablo had no sympathies for anyone from Caruna, he saw them as being the source of all his troubles. They had taken the money to build a new stadium while the small fishing village he lived in was hit by famine as the fish stocks dried up. He would have no trouble shooting any of these people who had ignored their problems.

Elna and Jan crept along beside the fence opposite the point where the checkpoint had been set up, until they were out of sight of the patrolling soldiers. Silently he motioned her to take the toddler in her good arm and hoisted himself over the fence, before landing noiselessly on the other side. Then he reached up as Elna passed the child over to him and he looked down on the sleeping bundle, praying it wouldn't wake, before turning his attention to helping her over. Then he led her up the hillside, watched by a herd of curious goats until they reached the tree line.

Having walked through the day they were all tired and could barely keep going but he wanted to get far enough before they rested so that the tree cover would keep them dry. After a while Elna tapped him and pointed towards a little stream and a spot where it looked well sheltered. He nodded and they scrambled down a little towards it. It was wet and all three of them were cold and hungry but he didn't dare light a fire, it would attract attention.

Elna watched him settle down on the ground and tried to get comfortable herself. She couldn't sleep, her arm hurt and she was worried about her brother, so she sat there cautiously peering into the darkness, praying that they wouldn't be found. After what seemed like hours of sitting motionless in the dark, the thunder started again. Throughout the day the rain had kept going. She wondered how the clouds could hold this much water but now lightning lit up the sky as well. As the flashes illuminated the trees around her she picked up her brother instinctively to keep him safe. Soon he was moving, the booms of thunder waking him. Jan too was beginning to stir. Then the child began to cry. He was here with his sister but he was cold, wet, hungry and the loud noises scared him. Jan suddenly sat up startled.

"If anyone hears that we'll be caught. Make him shut up!"

"I can't, it's the storm." Elna was trying to sooth the child, rocking him back and forth, hugging him tight so as to smother the sound. But still he wailed.

Pablo turned around, he could hear something in the distance. It was hard to make out between the claps of thunder but there it was again, faint, but definitely there. He sat down again, it sounded just like some animal. But there it was again and he wasn't so sure this time. He decided he had to investigate so, shouldering his rifle, he got up and set off in the direction it came from, pausing every now and then as the noise was drowned out by the storm.

As he came closer he became more and more certain that it was human. It sounded like somebody crying. But why would anybody be out here crying at this time, in this weather? Whatever reason, they shouldn't be here and it was his job to go and make sure they weren't, the only one anyone apparently thought he'd be any use at as he'd been here for two days now. He was starting to get annoyed that he'd seen so little of the actual fighting and hadn't done anything of much use. Well he might have to now, so he carried on, his bayonet leading the way.

By the stream, he pushed aside a few branches and looked down. The terrified faces of three children stared back up at him. They looked a sorry sight; a girl and a boy no older than 14, wet and dirty, the girl with one arm in a makeshift sling and a toddler, bundled up in soaking cloth, in the other. He had stopped crying now that he sensed the fear in his sister and clutched even tighter at Elna. She ignored the pain in her arm to hold him tighter and tried to make out the figure above them. He was just a silhouette, backlit occasionally by the lightning, but she could make out the steely glint of his rifle.

"You shouldn't be here."

"We know," Jan replied shakily.

"I should shoot you."

None of them had anything to say to that.

"I'm under orders to shoot anyone here. I can't let you go."

The children were frozen to the spot, paralysed with terror.

They were only children though, he thought. He should shoot them, he had no choice, but they were only kids. He scrambled down the bank to look them in the face but they cowered away from him into the shadows. Putting his finger to his lips he motioned them to be quiet, lowered his gun and turned his back. It was the bravest thing he'd ever done. It went against his belief that he should never disobey orders and if anyone found out he would probably be killed. But he couldn't shoot them.

Elna and Jan waited until his footsteps had disappeared and then looked at each other. Neither needed to speak, they both knew that they had to get away and gave up on the night's sleep. They hurried over the mountain. By dawn they were approaching Nine and Elna arrived just as her brothers and sisters were waking up. The baker and his wife smiled with relief, as their son and daughter reappeared, not uninjured but safe at least. Then they noticed the boy with her and wondered what had happened. They soon found out. Jan stayed with them for a couple of days and they treated him like a king but he had to go back and find his family.

The army reopened the road when they no longer needed it to be empty but they were still cautious that someone might try to set up a rebellion against the newly-formed government while it was still in its vulnerable infancy. It was for this reason that they were checking every traveller along it for weapons or anything else suspicious and Pablo had yet again been assigned to guard the pass. As Jan walked up the road towards the checkpoint they recognised each other. Their eyes met. Neither moved or showed any facial expression but the eye contact was enough and Pablo waved him on.

BETH TIMSON is 16 and lives in Sedbergh in Cumbria. The inspiration for Elna's War *came, she says, while "I was daydreaming. I kept thinking of images of these children and decided to write a story about them." Beth enjoys writing, acting and playing the flute. When she's older she wants to be a journalist and "write about real stories".*

The Deal

Karen Hands

I have been staring at the James Bond red digital numbers counting down long before the alarm goes off. Slowly I peel off the sweat stained sheets. I've had that dream again.

The cold pizza festering from last night stares at me with beady olive eyes. I feel sick. The smell of frying bacon makes my stomach rumble. I look blankly at the fat bubbling around the edge of the rashers. The images of the dream run through my head and cold sweat prickles down the back of my neck. I am only dragged from this horror by the faint smell of smoke. I look down and the bacon is a little crispier than I like.

I sit and eat staring at the crack in the wall that reminds me of someone I know. The man from the chip shop? The poodle from across the road? No. I think it's that girl who presents some late night TV programme.

Once the water runs off my body it doesn't look like water anymore. My three-day stubble makes me look like Clint Eastwood. The water trickles down my back and collects in a pool at my feet. The bathroom is cold so I put on my Calvins and a t-shirt. I leave my hair for that tousled look. Anyway, I've run out of gel.

Moving back to the lounge I have to move several weeks worth of newspapers to find the telephone. I dial the number from the scrappy piece of paper in my wallet.

"Hello?" Barry White is on the other end.

"Is that John?"

"No, I'll get him." The voice begins to sound more feminine. Must be his tart. Sounds like a man.

"Hello?"

"Hi John, it's me."

"Hi Pete."

"Have you got them?"

"Not yet. Soon. Don't worry, I'll have them before I see you."

"When? I really need them. I'm getting desperate here!"

"I said soon… there's no need to shout. It's not under my control. I've told you that before."

"OK, OK, I'm sorry. You know how I get carried away. But I'm getting really edgy here."

"Look, meet me at Fisher's on Castle Road."

"What time?"

"4 o'clock."
"Ah! 1600 hours."
"Get a life Pete."
"See you there." I put the phone down.

Outside the flat I meet the woman from 4b. She's wearing Prada with Gucci fuck-me shoes. A terrible mistake, so I don't want to. She tells me the bastard of a landlord is putting the rent up by £50. She flutters her eyelashes, I turn away bored. I ask to borrow £50. She gives it to me out of a wad of last night's earnings. She must have been busy. She knows I'll pay her back, I've never let her down before.

The stairs creak and groan on my way down. I walk to the bus stop, which is only about five minutes away. Even though it isn't open and I have just had my breakfast, the smell of curry wafting from the Rampant Rajah is very tempting.

Next bus to Castle Road is in half an hour, the timetable tells me. Sitting on the bench waiting, businessmen walk past in sharp suits, hair sleeked back, mobile phones chirping classical music they've probably never heard of. Their aftershave is so strong it gives me a headache.

The city is busy today. It makes me feel smaller and more alone than usual. The skyscrapers clawing their way up to block out the sun and the crowds with their asphyxiating crush. The bus arrives with its windows all steamed up and five minutes late.

There is no air. It's hot and smells like school science labs after sweaty first years have been in. My chest heaves visibly as I gulp in as much oxygen as possible. Heat creeps over my body and my neck to my face as I struggle to breathe. I fish my inhaler out and think calm thoughts: space and stars, the emptiness. But this just reminds me of the lack of oxygen.

It turns out that Castle Road is the last stop. As the journey goes on the bus slowly empties and soon I am the only person left. (I prefer this, as I am sure everyone was looking at me out of the corner of their eyes.

When I get off the bus I discover that Fisher's is a very dodgy looking café. I am 10 minutes early – meeting John seems like light years away.

Hyperventilating because of my need I walk into the bookshop two doors down. It is well stocked and I browse through the sci-fi/fantasy section. I am the only one there. A man in a long overcoat is looking at crime; he looks like a detective himself. A woman is paying for some children's books while her daughter covers a cardboard cut-out of the Naked Chef in sticky fingerprints. The middle-aged woman standing behind the till keeps checking on me, as if she thinks I might steal something. I have nowhere to put something without a bulge being obvious.

The smell when I eventually walk into the café is horrendous. There are various hot drinks, fried all-day breakfasts and numerous bad body odours that contribute to the overall mixture. John is sitting in the corner sipping at a coffee and looking very shifty. I walk over casually, trying to hide my fear and excitement. I have waited for this moment for an incredibly long time.

I long to hold them in my hands, to feel the power emanating from them, to feel that seeping through my body and take away my feeling of emptiness. I only hope John has them.

"Well?"

"I've got them, Pete."

"What...!" I almost shriek. "You've got them here... with you now?"

"That's right. I've had a Special Delivery since you telephoned me."

My hands start trembling the moment he says it.

"Who did you get them from?"

"You don't need to know. A friend."

"How much do I owe you?"

"£500. I would prefer it all now, but you could pay me in halves if you need to."

Getting the wallet out of my pocket is difficult, my hands are shaking so much. I have exactly the right amount, I was right to borrow that £50.

"Here you go."

"Thank you. A pleasure doing business with you. Now be very careful with them, and if I have anything else coming I'll let you know." He gives a wry smile as he slides the package across the table.

"I'd be grateful."

I walk hurriedly out of the café, and run as I see my bus at the stop. I am impatient to open the packet all the way home, but I do not want to spill its contents on the bus. As soon as I get home I sit on the sofa and carefully place the box on the table in front of me.

Gently I cut the string and slowly unwrap the brown paper. The box underneath has the seal on it. This is good shit. I take off the lid and there they are. As worn by Leonard Nimoy, a genuine pair of Spock's ears. I can die a happy man.

KAREN HANDS is 19 and lives in Arlecdon, a small village in Cumbria. She can't remember a time when she wasn't writing. She reads voraciously, especially books by Irvine Welsh, Terry Pratchett, Iain Banks and Donna Tartt. She plays bass guitar, loves the internet and has a "compulsive knitting disorder". Karen is currently studying media and communications and hopes that her future career can include creative writing of some sort.

Rocks of Utah

This land is wild,
Only the edge of the world
Could be so jagged.
This land is for the forsaken.
There is a lesson to be searched for in
This bareness.
These bloodless rocks,
Guardians of the word "never",
Dry of tears,
Beyond ignorance.
They are red in the arid air.
The sun has bleached them of all pity,
The harsh heat of truth
Burns even in their shadow.
They have survived.
Life is fought here, won,
Vision is the gift of this land.
The rocks bear their sharp crimson edges up to the sun,
All secrets laid bare.

Katherine Eyre

Station

Thinking about hot coffee and watching the smoke:
There's a poem being born here
Among the lazy, unlit corpses of cigarettes
And the tired random stares,
The uneasy expectation mired
Under lights bright enough to make this
Some haggard heaven.
Voices shuffle through distant traffic
And pick at the air.
The pounce of a sudden roar
Brings the train in,
Tearing the poem loose
In the rootless wasteland
Of never-ending destinations
Barely promised
By the silver glide of rails.

Katherine Eyre

KATHERINE EYRE is 19 and lives in Durham. She has written "since I could hold a pen" and is inspired by changes of scenery. Her other interests include fantasy fiction, philosophy, swimming, walking and watching cartoons.

Leeds

Leo Wilkinson

I go downstairs without brushing my teeth. In the kitchen, I take out my wallet and count my money. I have forty pounds and twenty pence. I try to find some food in the fridge. All there is, is beer. Grabbing my sleeping bag, jacket, wallet and keys, I close the door without making a sound. Outside it's fresh. The smell of bread from Gregg's bakery plays with my brain. I think about buying something but decide to save my money for Leeds. Up ahead, I see a sign for the train station. It's so early there are still people out from last night. A man like my father passes close to me. He's wearing a torn purple shirt and swigging from a can of Carlsberg Special Brew.

In the station, it's crowded. I wait for my ticket behind a man with a briefcase.

"Next."

I see an old grey head peering at me through the glass.

"One ticket to Leeds please."

"Speak up laddie."

"Leeds," I say.

"Single or return?"

That makes me stop and think. "Return, I guess."

"Thirty-nine ninety five."

"Thirty-nine ninety five?" I stammer.

"That's the price," she says.

I can see a queue forming behind me and someone yells, "Hey, kid."

I hand over forty pounds. I've got no money left.

"Change at York." She gives me the ticket.

I walk out onto the platform trying to stay cheerful. "I'm on my way to one of the greatest musical festivals ever," I say out loud. "Blink 192, Rage Against The Machine, Limp Bizkit. So what if I can't eat?"

The platform is dirty. It smells of some cleaning product that seems not to work. People push and shove. A pigeon snuffles around my feet then moves away towards the rubbish bin. Its feet make a sound. They are small and sharp as thumbtacks. I glance up at the station clock. The train is late.

"Any chance of a free drink due to the delay?" I ask a red-faced guard. He sneers at me. There's only twenty pee and five pence change from my ticket in my wallet. I move my sleeping bag from one arm to the other. My festival ticket and train ticket are safe in my jacket pocket. I close the zip.

One hour later, the train pulls into the station. By now the platform is crowded with commuters. I look at my ticket for a seat number. There isn't any number on my ticket. "Where do I sit?" I call to the same red-faced guard.

"Come with me," he says.

He takes me to the end of the train.

"Here you go lad." He leads me into a carriage full of rubbish from the buffet.

"What?" I try to complain, but he's gone and the train is already moving out of the station.

I sit down on the floor on my rolled-up sleeping bag. There are half-eaten sandwiches in the enormous bin liners, empty coke and beer cans and thousands of cardboard cups. I stare at a crushed beer can the size of my foot as it rolls towards the end of the carriage. It's 10am. The carriage smells of bad mayonnaise. "Why am I here?" I cry. "I paid forty pounds for a ticket. Forty pounds! And I'm thrown in here with the rubbish." There isn't even a window. I stand up, then I sit down again. There is a hole in the sole of my trainers that I can put my middle two fingers through. I think of my father's big fists; my mother and I hiding behind the settee. "I'm better off here," I say.

I spot an old issue of *Playboy* spilling out of one of the bins. I pick it out carefully. There's tomato sauce on the pages. I try to flick through them but they stick together. There is no centrefold. I read a boring story about Hugh Hefner's life.

The train stops. I don't know where we are. Then the Tannoy announces Darlington. I put down the magazine and take off my jacket. It is too warm in the carriage and there's tomato sauce on my fingertips. The smell intensifies.

As we leave Darlington, the door to my carriage opens and I see the red-faced guard show a drunk into my rubbish room. He turns away quickly and closes the sliding door with a slam.

"Where are you going?" The drunk stumbles then sits very close to me.

"Leeds."

"Fancy that." He winks at me perversely. He is very smartly dressed which I think is odd. I shuffle away from him. The bottom of my sleeping bag is filthy.

"I'm just back from Canada," he tells me. "Bear hunting."

"Oh yeah," I say.

His hands move in a nervous way. "It's chilly over there, but rewarding. The sight of bears in the wild making it..." He winks at me again. "You know, making it..." He sticks his index finger in the air and jabs it around, "was one of the best experiences in my life." He rubs his yellow hands together and drums his thick fingers on his knees. "And when they finished, I took aim and shot them." He takes a swig from a hip flask he pulls from his pocket. Then he offers the flask to me.

I shake my head.

"Where am I?" There's a long silence. Then I hear him snoring.

As the train slows I hear the announcement I've been waiting for. The next stop is York. I stand up. Then I notice the man's fat wallet. He's lying on his side and it's sticking half in and half out of his trouser pocket. I crouch over him. The wallet is oily brown. It makes a shuffling sound as I pull it between two fingers, touching it very lightly so it extends further out of the pocket. The old man doesn't move. The trains stops.

Without thinking I grab the wallet and run through the sliding door into the buffet car, then out the double doors where other passengers and the their luggage are waiting. "I have money," I think, touching the wallet which I've shoved in my jeans pocket. It is so big it makes my pocket bulge. "I have my train ticket and my festival ticket. I have my sleeping bag... and I have money."

The doors close behind me. On the platform, I follow other passengers to the Leeds train. I smirk when I see my old train departing the station. As I walk, I open the old man's wallet. Then I stop walking. The wallet is stuffed with bus tickets and receipts, but otherwise empty. I check all the compartments. There is no money.

Someone bumps into me. I cringe away. Just then, the connecting train to Leeds enters the station. I reach into my pocket for my ticket. Someone else bumps into me, jostling my shoulder. The pocket of my jeans is empty. I transfer the sleeping bag from one arm to the other. I look in the other pocket. Also empty, except for the wallet containing twenty five pence. I lurch to the wall. I'd left the train ticket and the festival ticket in my jacket. I look around. My jacket's on the train. All I have is the old man's wallet and my own. I left my jacket on the train.

Moving very quietly, I find a bench. I sit down for an hour, then I walk over to the phone box and ring my dad.

LEO WILKINSON is 20 and lives in Newcastle upon Tyne. His story was inspired by a visit to a music festival in Leeds. His interests include music, the writings of Irvine Welsh, Charles Bukowski and the films of Joel and Ethan Coen. He hopes to study English at university.

Bush Being Told – September 11th

Isn't technology great?
Only seven minutes wait
Since they used the planes against us
The news got through to Bush
He sat in Florida reading a book
To the children at school when he looks up
There is chief of staff, Andrew Card
Walking towards him, face stony and hard.
He leans down and whispers in the president's ear
Quietly so the children can't hear.
And suddenly the book is not on Bush's mind
As he stares and looks for words to find.
Shock, horror, disgust, alarm
Words not enough for the causers of such harm.
Thoughts and emotions running high,
Tears prick the president's eyes.
He stares, not at anything now
Over the shoulder of Card, wondering how?
Why? Why would someone do this?
You can see his anguish.
Lips thin, face pale, eyes showing pain.
I look at the picture again
Now it's not the president I'm seeing
But the face of an anguished human being.
A man whose eyes reveal all the grief
The sorrow, repulsion and disbelief.
Hundreds dead on impact, more to be revealed
Bush's eyes show all he feels.
An unpredictable event has shaken him as he was told
What had happened, images projected around the world.
The taste in his mouth must have been strong
The blood of the innocent, lingering for so long.
Events beyond his control yet control them he must
Through all the agony, suffering and disgust.
Bush must decide, choices must be made
He has to be diplomatic, his anger must fade.

But how can you tell a man his country has been attacked
And expect him not to fight back?
Revenge is natural, Bush must want that
But more lives lost in a destructive act?
His eyes may tell a tale but his mind must think
Can we avoid a war? Are we on the brink?
Technology may be great, but how we use it isn't
What happens now depends on a pensive president.

Joanne Shields

Too Far

The darkness is my comfort,
A haven from the light
I'm scared of the day
And I welcome in the night.
When the sun is in the sky
And I can feel its warmth
A tear falls from my eye
And my demons come to haunt.
People stalk my day
The crowds gather round
Images start to dance
And colours merge with sound.
A spit, a punch, a kick
They shout and scream with glee
Another in the ribs
From the bullies surrounding me.
A crowd, a gang, a mob,
Those who, I can tell
Have seen it as a duty
To make my life hell.
But one thing they cannot guess
Or else they would not gloat
Tonight I will be free
Tonight I slit my throat.

Joanne Shields

JOANNE SHIELDS is 15 and lives in Newcastle upon Tyne. She began writing when she was five and says that she continues to write because she "needs to". She is inspired by interesting people and enjoys reading and the cinema. In the future she hopes to become a writer.

The Mistake

Charlie Keys

The smog of the city destroyed the pallid red sunset and then clouded the night sky. The illumination from the dim streetlights shone on a select number of paving stones. Shadows made pictures of unearthly creatures on a canvas of derelict decrepit brickwork. A lonely disused feeling was potent in the uncompromising atmosphere. With the exception of the occasional silhouette of a disfigured rat, Granger Street was largely empty.

A figure moved at a steady speed round the corner past a boarded up greengrocer's. The shop had been abandoned several years ago but the familiar stench of unsavoury cabbage filled the nostrils of all who passed by. The figure paused for a second as the scent of the shop triggered an old memory, and then carried on walking, but his gait was decidedly slower. Where Oak Street finished and Granger Street began, a collaboration of the moon and a failing streetlight revealed the figure's appearance.

He was a short, skinny and undernourished man. His expensive suit jacket hung from his shoulders like a painting hangs from a wall. His shirt was new, tasteful and excessively dear. He had learnt the value of appearance soon after leaving university, that first impressions made a great difference in the city. But here in overcast suburbs he looked out of place. His face was worn and the lines of age spread prematurely across his pasty skin. The dark contours under his eyes were now a permanent feature.

His teeth were a clean white due to costly dental bills. And his hair, although fed with nutrients morning and night and cut every two weeks without fail, was more than starting to show the signs of age. He stopped again and took another glance at the greengrocer's, this time taking in more detail of the wooden sign above the rotting door. The paint was non-existent but at careful inspection the outline of letters was just visible. The chipped and scratched sign read 'Parker's Groceries'.

He didn't know why he had come back to Granger Street, let alone why he felt compelled to look at a shop. His old house, his old school, even the despised church, they all had some nostalgic value but his mind could not recall this place having any significance in his upbringing. He knew there was something he had overlooked. Maybe it was something he didn't want to recall.

He took a couple of paces down the deteriorated pavement. As he had no other thoughts to occupy his mind he meandered back towards the aged shop. Again he tried to remember. Some time passed in this street that never changes. Then it hit him. He wasn't sure whether the formidable sickness at the bottom of his stomach came before or after the memory. But the sickness definitely accompanied the memory.

He placed himself on the kerb, his brittle bony legs stretched out on the empty road. He was ten years old. His complexion was youthful and vibrant, and the only thing for him to worry about was his sunburnt nose and cheeks. His hair hadn't been cut all summer so his fringe covered his bright inquisitive eyes. He was wearing tattered jeans and a tee shirt which he knew was too large for him. He sat there on the stone steps. He recalled how pleasant it was to sit there as the sun's heat never seemed to reach them.

He'd spent a lot of his summer sitting on those steps, sometimes conversing with old people or rather listening to them. Most days there were teenagers on the street and he would watch them play football. But on the remembered day there were no old people and no teenagers. He recalled getting bored and letting his mind wander. He must have spent the best part of an hour daydreaming about what he was gong to do when he was older. He had imagined travelling around the world, even going to the moon. Now he had realised he had become none of the things he had dreamed of. In retrospect his ambitions were unrealistically high, but all of them would have been better than his present job. He was paid well; in fact people were jealous. But he still couldn't help feeling childishly ashamed of what he had become.

He took another look at the shop and then remembered back to that blistering summer's day.

After much daydreaming his thoughts moved to the present day. What could he do for excitement now? The young child's eyes looked and fell on the peaches, on a stand besides Parker's Groceries. The peaches in that shop were always palatable but on that hot day the sun was shining and the peaches were more vivid in colour. The temptation for their sweet nectar was unendurable. He had no money; he knew he could have gone home to get some, but he didn't. He felt he shouldn't have to.

He approached the shop with caution. For every step he took his heart rate seemed to increase. He could have stopped, but he didn't. He carried on until he was within grabbing distance. If he was going to steal, he would have to do it now. The shopkeeper would be back out of the stockroom at any moment. A part of him knew it was wrong. His hand clumsily grabbed the firm surface of the fruit and before he could think it was in his pocket. He started to walk away, afraid the shopkeeper would call after him; petrified anyone would call after him. But with every step he took away from the shop, every step towards the sanctuary of the stone steps, the more he wanted to get caught, the more he wanted to give back the peach. All he wanted was the guilt to disappear. Walking away from the shop he could almost see his mother's disappointed solemn face. He could hear the distressing shame that would be present in her voice, ringing in his eardrums.

He never did get caught, and he never returned the peach.

And for some peculiar reason he could now taste the sickly peach on the tip of his tongue.

The figure got up with an unhealthy amount of effort and walked back in the direction from which he had came. And the place where the two streets met fell empty and inanimate once more.

CHARLIE KEYS is 16 and lives in Hexham, Northumberland. Charlie has been writing for "as long as I can remember" and after A-Levels hopes to go to college to study either English or Film Studies. Charlie's short story was inspired by "the idea of someone looking back at something they regret", something that he feels many people can relate to. Charlie is inspired by "the people that I see around me".

The Beginning of the End

Emily Hudson

My mother was a piano teacher, she would not let me in the piano room, so I sat and listened at the door. She played beautifully, almost as beautiful as she was herself. I always thought it a pity that I did not look like her. Long, black hair (that, when tied back had tendrils still escaping) deep, brown eyes, that almost penetrated your very soul, and olive coloured skin. Now as I look back and write this, I am glad I did not.

I was like my grandmother, with short curly blonde hair, blue eyes and pinky white skin.

I grew up in a small Polish town, just a good little Catholic girl, no dreams of adventure. When I was quite small we heard of trouble in Africa. My daddy, a politician, went to help. Not wanting to be left behind, my mother and I followed.

My parents both got jobs in the government and I started my new school.

The conflict was solved and we settled down, living quite quietly for a few years there.

We befriended members of the Tutsi tribe. I saw friends marry and move on but nothing happened to me.

One day we were sitting on the veranda with my best friend Nansi and her family. We were listening to the radio when a message poured out of it like a river of hatred.

"All members or friends of the Tutsi tribe should be killed! They are all evil! Kill the Tutsis and live in a cleansed society!" Even if we didn't understand it then, we soon did.

A scream was heard down the street, gunshots fired. A huge truck came careering toward us. We ran to the only safe place we knew, the village church. I was terrified and I not only feared for my life but more for that of the actual Tutsi tribespeople. Fear turned my bones into speed and I flew.

Once all in we barricaded the doors and pulled the benches in front of them. We sat huddled together, women, children and grown men alike, shaking in fear.

Daddy had his gun, as did Nansi's daddy and some others.

We knew when they had arrived because they shot into the air, swearing in drunken voices, caught up in the madness, the fever of the moment.

They broke the doors down... they broke the benches down... And then they broke my daddy... I remember the look on my mother's face as my daddy's head rolled on the floor.

I ran forward and grabbed my daddy's gun. BANG! One fell dead RETRIBUTION. BANG! Two dead JUSTICE. BANG! Three dead VENGEANCE.

As men died, women took their weapons - guns, machetes and even farming tools. But to no avail. Some were raped so violently they died. Others were left with something worse.

Eventually we were subdued. There were forty of us left, including six children. Nearly all of the women, including Nansi, had been raped. All the men were dead.

I was distraught; my mother lay on the ground, her beautiful piano hands twisted above her head where they had held her. Her hair was torn and messed where she had twisted trying to escape her rapist. I soon realised she was dead. Her hands would no longer play.

They did not seem to see me behind my pew. I grabbed a young child's hand and we ran quietly to where a heap of benches lay, we put blood on us from the wounded to make it look as if we were dead and hid in the benches. I closed my eyes and the child followed suit. Slash, scream. Slash, scream. The tendons were cut in each person's legs so that they could not run away, they didn't do it to us though. We were so relieved we cried; I just held her to me singing an old lullaby. The fear had paralysed us. We were frozen in our positions of terror.

When the soldiers had left I crawled out and helped those I could, many died from loss of blood.

It was six days before the child and I ventured out. An American army truck pulled up. They thought I was one of their soldiers. They took us in, the little girl and me. We were two of a handful of survivors from a huge massacre. I left Africa with the intention of never going back.

We were saved but most were not so lucky. The women who were not killed that day now have to handle something far worse, AIDS. You see, when the soldiers raped them they did not have to kill them, AIDS would do that. The soldiers knew they had this disease and now most of their victims are dead. The Tutsis are dying out. I knew that if I went back I would be haunted by what I had seen, but it doesn't matter because it wakes me screaming anyway. The faces of those who murdered my parents are amongst them.

The men who committed these awful murders were imprisoned and are hated by many; I however do not hate them. They were led by evil men, but what they did was not in their power because they were brainwashed by propaganda and their leaders.

As I write this I realise that I must go back to Africa and let my demons go.

As I step off the plane I see familiar sights but I don't feel like crying. I call a taxi and we drive to my old village. I see women sitting outside houses chatting, sewing and cooking. This is not how I left it five years ago. But as I look closer I see something strange, there are no men, I see boys but no men. I go faster to my house, tears pouring down my face, and I see a woman lying on a bed, Nansi. She sits up and smiles at me. She is frail and does not look her age.

"Phoebe?" Her eyes shine with tears. It is a miracle she has been saved! But some fear clings on at the back of my mind. This may be the end for Nansi.

"Yes Nansi, I'm here." We sit and hold each other, united at last. And in these moments I know Nansi will die. We cry and laugh; remembering the life I had left. Nansi stands up and I see that she has huge marks on her knees. She smiles as I stare.

"That is where they cut, remember?" I nod with no words to say.

"It was not within your power to stop them." How could she know what I had been thinking? I'd always blamed myself for what had happened then, and now I let it go. It wasn't my fault; I couldn't have done anything. Nansi stumbles and falls, I rush to catch her. As she stops breathing, I start to howl, I miss her so much. I stumble out of the house, tears blind me. I hear myself calling that she is dead, that she died in my arms, then someone tells me that Nansi died five years ago. "No," I say. "Her body's in there", trying to convince them, trying to convince myself. But when I walk back in there is no body. The house is empty, it smells musty but is deserted. It had been for a long time now. But if it wasn't Nansi who was it, the person who had helped me let go of my demons? I was thinking my life had ended that day but it had only just begun.

More than 800,000 people were massacred in the ethnic conflicts in Rwanda in the 1990s, leaving the survivors to try to rebuild their lives and the people and possessions they lost.

EMILY HUDSON is 13 and lives in Jarrow in South Tyneside. Her story was inspired by a documentary about the Tutsis which was shown on television as part of Comic Relief. Emily is inspired by "people, such as Nelson Mandela, who have been put through great ordeals and can still find it in their hearts to forgive those who carried out the act". She hopes to become a lawyer and to continue to write in her spare time.

Be aware of how we work

If you make my fiery
Belly butterflies flutter and flounce
Their pretty painted wings;
Come closer.

If you hear nothing but
Mothy pitter-patters;
Don't bother.

If you see a flame burn
Golden in my eyes;
Then love me.

If you see a hollow
Cold igloo stare;
Please leave,
Silently.

When a frog hops in my throat
And chokes me;
Relax with me.

When life's hard lines
Hook me,
Be strong for me.

When all the cold space
Is around me
Hold me,
Just hold me.

When the world's wicked tongues
Devour you;
Ask for me
Just ask for me.

Roxie Willows

ROXIE WILLOWS is 21 and lives in Hexham, Northumberland. As well as developing her poetry skills at open mic events on Tyneside, she also writes song lyrics and puts them to music. She loves travelling and has just returned from four months in America. Her main influences are the Beat poets and writers such as Allen Ginsberg and Jack Kerouac and she is inspired by "the surreal and obscure" and by the "purity and complexity of animals and nature".

African story

Hannah Glancy

It's 1965, one year since Zambia became independent and as things slowly change two young girls watch each other...

It's as if honey oozes out of her head I think as I gaze on through the mesh. So perfect, every strand shimmers in the sun, glinting gold like a halo.

I shift uncomfortably in my itchy ensemble of clothes and gaze longingly at her fine dress which must have cost a considerable amount; well maybe not to her as there is no shortage of wealth in her family, which is a strong flowing river of riches.

The possibility of lingering here all day is not one open to me, so I turn away to a hard day's toil.

I observe her depart and am relieved. Her staring stoical face was unnerving and I could hardly bear it any longer.

She is in a deplorable state, I think, as she goes to sweep the veranda of our neighbour's fine house. She lives in a petite one-room house pronounced 'Kyah'.

Though her situation is dire, she is not without a certain beauty. Sometimes I wonder if her skin would be as smooth as chocolate to touch, whether her hair is springy and wiry or soft and fuzzy. She has big, brown, benevolent eyes. She fascinates me.

My tenderhearted mother teaches the local girls who had to leave school at fourteen but who want to further their education; I suppose they learn something. Mother encourages us to mingle with them, but her job is increasingly difficult since father died.

Sunset is my favourite time of day. I love the sun's balmy glow as it wishes goodnight and withdraws into a sea of amber to make way for a blanket of indigo in which stars appear twinkling mischievously.

I hope I have done justice to describing my most treasured time of day. My English has been coming along well I think and I wish to learn as much as I can so I can write. I left school at fourteen so it has been hard to get further education apart from the kind lady next door.

Elsie is in the garden again, I would love to meet her, but I cannot because it's not my place and I know my place all right.

I glance over at Elsie again and notice her shoes, they are the new Mariposas; I instantly adore them and wish I had a pair.

"All the colours of the rainbow are in that store!" exclaims Lydia every time we pass it on the high street. But why Elsie has chosen lime green will forever be a mystery, sky blue would have fitted her blanched complexion and suited her icy blue eyes much better. I feel an urge to go and tell her, maybe I will...

Oh no, she's ambling over this way. What on earth do I say?

"I love your Mariposas, but wouldn't sky blue be more your colour?"

I gape at her open mouthed, I'd wanted that colour but my girlfriends had coaxed me into lime green like them.

"They have all sorts of colours: gold, orange, cherry, scarlet, rose, pink and violet... the list could go on to infinity. My favourite is silver though; I love them, I really do. Anyway, look at me babbling on, I've lots of chores to do before dinner time and I must go help mamma make our meal."

She dashes off and I shout goodbye after her, not actually remembering her name until she was out of sight, I think it's Kasondi.

I spoke to her and she seemed sweet, I hope we meet again. A friendship is not likely, although it would be nice to have someone to talk to over the fence. I wish we could all get along without us being treated as though we're not their equals and we're below them.

Reflecting on yesterday's conversation, I am beginning to think maybe they are human after all and the same as us. Besides, Kasondi is quite as sweet as my mother keeps insisting.

Next door there are shouts. The poor girl is being told off for not doing jobs either quick enough or well enough. Now I feel guilty for treating Carmen, our maid, much the same way.

Carmen is ill and we have hired a temporary maid to do the work. I think I might visit Carmen this afternoon.

I sit back and sip some lemonade, but instantly feel awful in my cool light summer clothes. Kasondi slaves away in that shapeless cloth which she refers to as clothing. I want to get to know her better.

Ten times I have scrubbed this floor and each time Mrs Sandstone has been angered with me.

"It must sparkle like a diamond before tonight or I will cut your wages.

Clean it ten times more and scrub ten times harder!" she screeches at every possible chance.

As you can see she is in excellent spirits for her extravaganza tonight. She claims important people are coming though she never says who. I expect it's a few of the richer neighbours and a couple of friends who are all white and much luckier than me. Anyway if she cut my wages I'd be working for free!

My dress now resembles the cloth that I have been using to scrub the floor and so I am not surprised when she hires white servants to serve the food, all of whom are given uniforms.

She suggests a new dress might be handy for me. Ha! We don't have enough money for food, let alone a new dress.

After this excruciating morning I am to have a lesson with Mrs Millefeuille, Elsie's mother, my highlight of the day. I will learn something more than how to make a floor sparkle. I cannot wait to leave I think, as I enter the dingy, dark, damp bedroom for a scouring session.

"What does alliteration mean?" my mother asks, peering into the faces of her six attentive students.

Kasondi meekly raises her hand and endeavours to answer "Is it a series of words starting with the same letter?"

This is obviously the right reply as my mother gives a mountain of praise, to which Kasondi reacts by beaming contentedly with a smile. I suspect she may want to be a teacher.

I sit silently at the back, perceiving every move, examining every sound. It's a long two hours but when the lesson finally ends I grab Kasondi for a chat.

"I took your advice on the shoes and I think they're great. How did you know blue would've been better?" As soon as I say this her eyes swivel downwards and a reply slips out but I don't quite catch it. She then starts to exclaim ecstatically how much she loves them and how they suit me so.

Deeper matters of discussion appear in our discourse and presently I invite her to dinner, which she accepts. At that instant I decide I like her and she is enjoyable to be around, she is a brilliant friend, who is vibrant and enthusiastic (plus she says she will do my hair in special plaits and braid it).

Yesterday's meal was sumptuous and I had a really good time. I'm lucky to have a friend like Elsie. I admire her new shoes and value the fact that she took my advice; friendship suddenly is a possibility. I enjoy talking to her and at the moment am elated to have her as my neighbour.

She adored the way in which I did her hair, braided with bright beads. We had a cheery giggle when her brother, all dressed up to go on a date, slid into the pool by accident and we had to fish him out. It was hilarious.

I think Kasondi is right about the shop being filled with mini rainbows as I pause to look at it whilst on the high street. My eyes slither over to the metallic silver pair and instantly I recall Kasondi's face lighting up as she talked about them. I wonder how long she has spent admiring them but never being able to buy her very own. About to turn away I reach into my pocket and feel the kuacha notes there... just enough!

Glinting and glimmering in the sunlight I gaze down at them, I can't believe they're mine and I embrace her again. Lost for words all I can do is hug her and even though I don't say it, I think she knows how much I love them. I quietly promise to always be her friend and I think she understands as she whispers, "I promise too." A tear of bliss drops to the ground where I glimpse them again; my very own gleaming silver Mariposas...

Hannah Glancey is 14 and lives in Endmoor, Cumbria. Her story is inspired by her mother's stories of her childhood in Zambia, but "if I find something that interests me, or I think makes a good story, I will write about it". She particularly enjoys writing "when it's raining". In the future, Hannah would like to "help the people of Africa and live in Spain".

A Different Time

On a night like many others
The world lay beneath
A heavy cloud cover.

Winds swirled in the atmosphere
And the blanket flapped,
        Yet she lay on in the darkness
Under covers.

The movements stopped
        Stillness descended
Stifling her. Silently
Until no more air seemed to exist in the darkness.

Suddenly something stirred –
Reminding her of a different time –
And the
Wind prevailing
        Sent petals
                Cascading from green
                      Away to below
Where they were caught and saved
Quickly
Before being lost on harsh rocks.
Their fragile shapes floated upwards...
This new breeze loved them   and they bounced,
Splashed in the sky's rolling surf.

The petals effortlessly parted waves
Of turbulent seas
Revealing stars burning
More brightly it seemed, than ever
And for a moment,
A different time
        from before
                was
Hers again.

She awoke abruptly from her slumber –
Contented thoughts surprised her now –
And as she   stepped   from   airless   dreams
Eyes
        searched skywards frantically
Clawing and grasping to hold on.

Eyes
Opened to this brighter glow
Glimpsed within stars a light from the past.

But it was torn and ripped and no longer comprehensible.
And when the clouds rolled in
Useless
It was extinguished
        And drowned
                In watery

        Depths.

Jodie Gray

JODIE GRAY is 17 and lives in Morpeth, Northumberland. She began writing when she was very young and would like to eventually have a job which allows her to travel the world, ideally a travel writer. Her poem was inspired by her love of the sky, especially at night: "I was struggling to sleep and so sat at my window and was greeted by a very dramatic and exciting sky at night." She is inspired by explorers and "those who discover new places and travel to unexplored wildernesses".

The One Who Destroys

Slither like a snake,
Fly like an eagle,
Creep like a fox,
Watch the owls as they wake,
See the king, the lion, so regal,
Copy the parrot as it mocks,
Be the rabbit, jumping for joy,
Or...
Be you –
The one who destroys.

Stephanie Fisher

We Have Rights

I sit quietly,
Waiting,
Staring,
My friends, my family and my foe,
They are no more.
Lives destroyed,
Habitats devastated,
The bush burns red and amber.
Through the smoke,
I can see a machine,
It echoes through the darkness,
Strange to my world
I can hear the buzz of weapons you creatures use,
And the sound of majestic trees, thundering to their death.
When will you creatures learn?
The environment should not be destroyed.
We are animals.
We have rights.

Stephanie Fisher

STEPHANIE FISHER is 14 and lives in Barrow in Furness. She has always written stories and began to write poetry two years ago. Her poems are inspired by her love of animals and in the future she hopes to become a primary school teacher and to continue to write. She admires JK Rowling and would "love to write children's books like her".

Down Comes Rain

Helen Fairgrieve

I'm walking down the corridor again, breathing that hospital smell of disinfectant and pain. Suddenly you start calling for me but I can't find you, there are too many doors and not enough time. There's never enough time. The end of the corridor is getting further and further away. It doesn't matter how fast I run, I know I'll never reach the end but I'll keep running, I promise you I won't stop. I wake up screaming. Again.

The sky is still smothered in clouds, the sun hasn't dared to show its face but it hasn't rained yet. It's humid and warm, the type of weather that lets you know that thunder and rain are never far away. It's confusing the cat.

I need to get out of this house; I decide to wander towards the park. The flowers look up to me expectantly and the birds sing their secret hymns while the sun hides behind heavy clouds. The grass stretches before me like a thick carpet and the river slides gracefully by: it all appears in silent monochrome, my thoughts are full of you.

I sit curled up with a warm drink and Tabitha on my lap, listening to her comforting purr. I remember you let me buy her because you thought she was entertaining, a meringue with an expression you said, an absurd crossbreed, an amusing hybrid, an abnormality to keep us company. I don't need photographs to keep you real; it's times like this that you come to me. My thoughts are clearer than photographs anyway, they're more faithful to you and in them, you still move.

I remember the first time I met you, I was nervous of you simply because you were the most beautiful thing I had ever seen. The music seemed to be getting louder and I knew the alcohol was going to hit me. My inhibitions flew away over the bar, over the rows of sparkling spirits in their bright, bright bottles and out, out into the night air to hide among the stars. I came over and asked you if I could buy you a drink. I woke the next morning, cradled like a newborn in your arms, the smell of vomit in my hair. Why bother with the memories of innocent romance? This means so much more.

This time I'm moving through the air, slowly and tentatively, cautious because I know this feeling won't last. I'm not going to waste it by greedily tumbling and turning through the sky, I just want to be. I glide slowly past clouds, I feel graceful, like a dancer - slim and nimble, exquisitely elegant. Suddenly, although I knew it was going to happen, I'm falling quickly and I can't stop myself. I wake again and it's six o'clock, Tabitha needs to be fed.

Since they made me take a break from work I've had nothing to do. I take naps through the day because I can't rest at night. I've been given something to help me sleep but I don't want to take it, if it's not meant to be, it's not meant to be; you said. No more.

For the first few nights I tried; took a long bath, had a warm drink, listened to that 'lift music' I've always hated. Now I've given up. Instead, I glide through time and space, night by night, working through the shelves of books we bought but never had time to read. I've watched murders with a calm confidence, cried for the dying and mourned for the dead; I've visited foreign lands, tasted fruit with my eyes and found my soul mates living hundreds of years away.

I might go next door to May's for a change of scenery. I'll have to wait until I can stomach that bad taste mix of floral patterns that makes my head ache, and the nauseating smell of mothballs. We'll have a nice cup of tea and I'll listen to the unimportant stories about friends: Mrs Anderson's new hip, her prize cats and Maggie's misbehaving son, the uninteresting chatter that takes my mind away from everything else. I find myself wondering why she keeps moving around the room. I notice that she's continually relocating her china treasures to new homes. Why is she avoiding sitting near me? I suppose crying does always make her nervous, she doesn't like it because she doesn't seem to know what to do. Hugging me seems to be too personal for her but she can't just sit by, so she pats me delicately instead. Like an animal, like I'm always just about to break.

I'm in a box and I can't get out. Classic. It's getting smaller and I can't breathe, someone is shutting me in but I can't see their face, they're wearing a surgical mask, green but not green. It's not grass or leaves, not moss or ferns but it's still green, a fraud, a manmade imitation. I've given up fighting now, it's dark and my box is shut, there's no way out and no one to hear me call. I wake sweating to hear Gene Kelly's 'Singing in the Rain' on the radio. You liked that one, a prime example of how men don't think about the consequences of what they do. If you really sang in the rain for that long you would probably just get pneumonia. You knew all the words though.

I watch films too, but never the same one twice, I wouldn't be able to see them all that way. I restrict myself to watching the delicious films that offer us a slice of culture, subtitled films, sometimes Japanese, mostly French. I write you poems, then I light the fire and watch them float slowly upwards to the sky in the heat, as in *Mary Poppins*. Not only because it gives me the chance to indulge myself in something madly childish but also because they're too bad to read out loud and I'd be embarrassed if I picked them up again. I loved all the childhood classics, *Mary Poppins*, *The Railway Children*, *Chitty Chitty Bang Bang*; they made you laugh because you were so cynical. You said it was just another way of disillusioning children, cars didn't fly, nannies aren't magical and you don't ever get away with stealing vast amounts of coal. You called me a sad case for needing them and their escapism. You haven't left me anything.

Some of my dreams are more like memories, of the moments I realised how much we cared for each other. My favourite is from the time when I arrived home from work and you weren't in the house, in the study, the kitchen. Not knowing where you were made me panic and I called your name out over and over. I ran to the garden and saw you, sitting with one leg resting on your completed pages to stop them from chasing the moving air; the other outstretched near a leaning tower of books. Your eyes tearing through page after page of war, destruction, desperation and broken tears of rage. The sun shining on your face, lighting up your hair like a halo and the breeze blowing your skirt out indecently, like Marilyn's. The boundaries between you and the light blurred as if you were an illusion. I sat and watched you for a while before you noticed and dashed towards me with that secret look that meant you missed me. Loved me.

Then it hit me that you weren't coming back, not now, not ever. I felt a wave of panic and begged for reality, to feel, to hear, the phone to ring. The ground reached skyward to catch me clumsily between its outstretched arms.

Finally the rain came; sitting in the window seat watching the drops slip past the panes, tears fell from my face, imitating those from the sky. That night I slept.

HELEN FAIRGRIEVE is 17 and lives in Morpeth, Northumberland. She is inspired by family, friends, "my Marc" and by all of the poetry and prose that she reads. After university, which begins next year, she hopes to work in a career involved with writing or publishing.

Bounce

A ball does not love
to bounce
against hard ungiving ground,
to fly
between inconstant fingers.
Does not love
the rise, the fall,
and rejection repeated from hand to hand.

The ball loves
the moment of catch and caught:
suddenly
not plastic
not shiny
but a crumpled mess of feathers.
A baby bird.
Safe in two cupped palms –
the warm deep dark,
the safe sphere.

Longing to be lost,
longing for the deep
and the dark
of the toy cupboard:
there to be forgotten
one final time, no more.
There to imagine
hands which don't force flight:
the forever caught
of the padded palm-cell.

Dave Rinaldi and Briony Chown

Thankyou

I've stopped wanting to kill you.
When you left
I dreamt you'd been
stoned to death
with chocolates,
or crushed
by cuddling teddy bears
or smothered
with rose petals
or wrapped up and bound with string
out of sight, immutable and alone.

But chocolate melted
in my fingers
and all my dreams run from me
like ink messages
scrawled on warm palms
or wine through water.

When you left
You left beautiful scars
which slice up my heart
and will never heal
(for which I am inexpressibly grateful).

Dave Rinaldi

DAVE RINALDI is 21 and is from Sunderland though he is currently studying at the University of Sheffield. He wrote the poem Bounce *with BRIONY CHOWN. They have both been involved with creative writing for a while and are inspired by "late night conversations after dancing". They also enjoy photography, soul music, the films of the Coen brothers, early morning sunlight, train journeys, mountains and beaches. When they leave college they both want to work either with a fair-trade organisation or for an international development charity.*

By Blood, By Fire

Ruth Gilfillan

It was a cold night. Countless stars glittered in the velvet sky like crystal droplets of scattered water, clear and sharp even in the bright light of the full moon. A perfect disc of white gold, its cold light glinted off the waters of the pounding sea, shattered, and was reflected in a thousand silver splinters. But the moon's steady glow was not the only light that illuminated the sea, the sheer cliff face and the rugged countryside: only yards away from the drop, a fire burned, and in front of it, facing each other, stood a man and a woman.

The firelight danced over the man's face - a handsome one with pale skin and dark eyes - forming a hellish halo around his sable hair. The fire was nothing compared to the flames of anger burning in his eyes. The focus of his wrath was the young woman who faced him with her back to the fire.

She was beautiful, with eyes as green as leaves in spring and hair as red as leaves in autumn, but the hate in her face made her ugly. She wore a floor length orange wool dress with a scarlet cords tied around her waist, but on her dress were stains - blood stains. Her hands were also flecked with dried blood. A ring on her finger was her only ornament save for a pattern of blue woad tattooed round her neck and neither the gold of the ring nor its blood-red gem were discoloured. If the woman's clear green eyes were the window to her soul, then her soul was twisted and corrupted with hate and malice.

The pale moon looked down on the scene and saw how easily the woman, who had murder in her eyes, could simply reach out and push the man off the cliff.

The woman spoke, her eyes still fixed on those of the man. "No. I will not forget. I will not forgive. Even when I am dead, I will not be gone. My blood will remember, Pwynedd. My blood will remember."

And she stepped backwards into the flames.

She died silently. Even as her hair and clothes began to burn, her expression did not change. She did not even wince, but continued to hold the man's eyes in her gaze.

And when the roaring flames had consumed her body, and the wood had turned to ash, only her ring remained, glowing blood-red with an internal fire.

"Hey, look at this!" said Hope. "*Celtic Crime and Punishment*." She opened the book at random and read a section. "This might help."

Hope took the heavy book to her best friend, Jayne, who was sitting at a table that was barely visible under piles of books, pictures and print-outs on Celtic history and legends. The girls were researching for a history project on the mythology and customs of the Celts, but there was a problem. They had left their research quite late, and most of the useful books in their local library on the subject had already been borrowed.

Jayne pushed her red hair out of her face and looked up at her approaching friend. "What?"

Hope laid the book on the table and pointed to a section. Jayne read it aloud. "If a man had an affair with a woman, his wife could kill that woman without punishment. However, this sentence had to be carried out within three days. One account tells us of such a case, where the husband, the wealthy Pwynedd ad Myrr chased his wife Yrair to the coast.

"Historians are divided over what happened next: some say Pwynedd pushed her off a cliff and some say she took her own life in the same way. One source claims that Yrair was a witch, and that she conjured up a fire and burnt herself in it, cursing her husband."

There was an illustration with the story: a dark-haired, dark eyed man |with pale skin stood facing a red-haired, green-eyed woman who had her back to a roaring fire. The woman had her arms upraised, and the picture had been cleverly drawn so that the light of the full moon glinted off the ring on her hand. Jayne gazed at the scene, tracing the shape of the blazing fire with a finger.

"Jayne?"

Jayne shook herself out of her reverie. "Yeah, it's great." She made a few notes, but then glanced at Hope. "Look at the picture. "Hmm... do you think? I think you look like Yrair – hey, your ring even looks like hers!"

Frowning, Jayne looked at her ring. "Mm-hmm..."

Neither of them spoke for a while. Hope broke the silence by shutting the book with a snap. "Right." She checked her watch. "The library closes in five minutes. I'll take this out and then we'll clear up."

The girls said goodbye outside the library gates. Just before they were out of earshot, Hope turned and yelled: "Jayne, remember it's camping tonight! I'll see you at Fay's at 7.30!"

Smiling, Jayne gave her the thumbs up, and continued walking.

Nine o'clock that night saw Jayne and Hope sitting round an unlit camp fire outside a tent in their friend Fay's garden, along with a nearly empty bottle of Coke, a pick 'n' mix from their local sweet shop and a lot of wrappers.

The fire was piled high with crumpled newspaper but the branches still refused to ignite, even though there was no wind and the fuel was dry.

"Here, let me try." Fay took the matches off Hope and tried again. The match flared and Fay touched it to the paper which started to smoke. Strangely, Jayne felt a sudden sense of foreboding. The trio held their breaths. The match flickered and went out. Another try. Another feeling of dread. Another failed attempt.

A breeze rustled through the night, sending chills up Jayne's spine.

The girls were down to their last match. As Fay struck it on the side of the box Jayne glanced up at the sky to see the full moon glide out from behind a cloud.

"Yesss!"

Jayne looked back at the fire. It was alight.

An echo of a scream...
A chill like ice...
The smell of burning hair...
The taste of fire...

Jayne felt a whirling sensation and suddenly everything was wrong. The house, the garden and the tent were gone and all that was left was the fire, grown to over six feet high, burning on what was now a cliff. Fay had disappeared and Jayne and Hope were alone.

Nearly alone.

Out of the fire stepped a tall figure, red-haired and green-eyed. Clothed in an orange dress she stood motionless and looked Jayne straight in the eyes.

"I have returned."

The shadow of Yrair paced slowly forward and when she reached Jayne she did not stop. Hope, watching, saw that Yrair seemed to dissolve into Jayne's ring, and then Jayne's face changed, becoming harder, sharper and older. When the moonlight caught her clothes, they seemed to change to the orange dress and flicker between this and the jeans and coat which Jayne had been wearing.

The ring glowed blood-red.

Jayne-Yrair advanced on Hope. "I have kept my promise, Pwynedd! I have returned to eliminate your blood from this world – and I will start with this girl!"

Even in her near-petrified state, Hope had the presence of mind not to back away as she would have fallen over the edge of the cliff. Instead she ran around Jayne-Yrair and past the fire. Now she was in little danger of being pushed into either the sea or the fire.

Thoughts ran through Hope's head as Jayne-Yrair advanced and she looked around to find something with which she could defend herself. There was nothing, nothing that she could use as a weapon. She scooped up some sand and threw it at Jayne-Yrair's face. It missed.

Now Hope was desperate. Frozen to the spot with fear and confusion, she watched helplessly as Jayne-Yrair came towards her. Hope watched as the mental battle continued, hardly daring to breathe lest she break Jayne's concentration. At last, Jayne wrenched the ring off her finger and Yrair's spirit left her but did not disappear. Jayne's face cleared but she still looked confused and disorientated.

"Here!" cried Hope, holding her hands out. Jayne threw the ring to her. Now Hope dodged past Yrair and ran, pursued by the shade, hoping that she would reach the cliff edge before Yrair caught her. She passed the fire and slid to a halt only feet away from the drop. Raising her arm up and back, she hurled the ring with all her might into the sea.

"Noooooooooo!"

Yrair's scream of fury was terrible, made clearer and sharper by the cold winter air. When the ring touched the water, Yrair's shadow vanished leaving only...

An echo of a scream...
A chill like ice...
The smell of burning hair...
The taste of fire...

And everything was back to how it was. The house, the garden and the tent had returned and the campfire was small and newly lit. Fay looked puzzled as Hope and Jayne looked wildly around and exchanged confused glances.

"What?" she said

Jayne blinked "I... nothing". Mentally, she shook herself. *That can't have happened – can it? Anyway, even if it has, Fay would never believe me if I told her. Best just to ignore it and try to forget about it.* "Come on, let's toast some marshmallows."

Many years later, a red-haired teenager was walking along the shore, a border collie sniffing around at her heels. It was late evening. Something caught her eye.

Lying among the pebbles and shells was a golden ring, its blood-red stone oddly smooth and unscratched. It reflected the full moonlight, corrupting it so that it seemed almost as if a fire were burning within its sinister depths.

The full moon looked on as the girl bent to pick it up, examined it and slipped it on her finger.

An echo of a scream...
A chill like ice...
The smell of burning hair...
The taste of fire...

RUTH GILFILLAN is 14 and lives in Morpeth, Northumberland. She began writing when she was nine and has enjoyed creative writing at school ever since. In the future she would like to work either in psychology or to follow her Christian beliefs and be a missionary. Ruth is inspired by the scenery and people of Northumberland, history and by current events. In her spare time she enjoys reading, watching TV and swimming. Her favourite authors are Terry Pratchett and JRR Tolkien.

Tramp

Georgina Ascroft

She sits waiting in a chair for her mother to finish making her tea. The room is quiet, with the flickering television on mute. She sighs deeply and closes her eyes, soaking up the atmosphere of warmth and love.

In this living room are a sofa and her grandmother's rocking chair. The adjoining dining room has a table of plain wood design, filled with piles of coursework belonging to her older brother. The chairs don't match but she loves it.

She loves the little china clowns and strange shoe ornaments that belonged to mum when she was a girl. She loves the squashy sofa. Though the springs are broken it is great fun to sink into it in the winter when the gas fire is smoking its little heart out. She opens her eyes again as the smell of sausages drifts up her nose. She sighs and gazes out of the front window.

It's raining. She smiles. She loves the rain too, it make her feel glad to be inside, snuggled up and warm. The people outside hurry along, their umbrellas up and coats pulled tightly across to protect them. She observes their comings and goings. wondering idly what kind of lives they have. A car zooms past and sprays pedestrians. She giggles. But something catches her eye which makes her stop. A man is out there, obviously homeless. "Tramps" her father calls them, but her mother says not to call them names, you must feel sorry for them. So she does, and tries to imagine a new, nice and happy life for the poor man.

"Dinner!" calls her mother. She jumps up and runs into the kitchen, leaving the quiet place and the man on the pavement across the street.

He lies still, silent and cold beside an open gutter. The plastic pipe has split and a steady gush of drain water from the house spurts over his head like a fountain. Great puddles of it foam around him, and then with the cold wind, they fly like wild birds, in all directions.

Half a cone of chips sits forlorn, sagging and measly next to the man, wrapped loosely in sodden newspaper. The ink is running down from the paper, dripping off, collecting on the ground, then with a splash of water it is all whooshed down into the gutter.

Rain dribbles down his grimy face, off his nose and chin, down his beaten forehead onto his clothes.

He stares, transfixed by people as they pass him by. Their feet are splashing in the rain water. Time seems to slow; it becomes sluggish while he lies hypnotised, watching the feet in fancy shoes fly across the water.

Droplets are flung outwards, spraying the broken flagstones. The man doesn't move as water is splashed and flicked in his face. He doesn't see it, or feel it. For the cold has slowly crawled along his body, leaving a rotten trail of dull, grey numbness.

He doesn't hear the sound of the local thugs, laughing, jeering at him, throwing hard jagged stones and empty beer cans to shift him.

Not that he can. No, he will continue to lie there beneath the house, soaking up more dirt as time goes by. His clothes are thin with time and his worn through shoes are lost somewhere. A cheap baseball cap is jammed on his head, and a beaten watch which had long since stopped ticking is banded to his arm. He stares, long and away.

A small boy is whimpering in his cot. He clutches a ragged chew toy to his chest and cowers in a corner. The spindly bars of the cot tower over the boy, making him shrink deeper into the headboard with fear. A part of the board is broken off and his leg hangs helplessly out, caught on the jagged edge. He dare not look. He screws his eyes shut to avoid seeing the cold bare room around him. A siren wails outside, tearing through the boy's ears. The lights of the ambulance cut through the thin curtains that hang limp and lopsided on the rail. A bitter wind flings itself through the broken glass pane and rushes round the room making him prickle and shiver.

The dingy wallpaper is peeling off, revealing cracked plaster and brick, and the damp wooden floor is slowly being eaten away by woodworm. To the side of the room lying very still is a mangy looking thing, and yet this is what the boy pines for as he sits alone in the crumbling room. His little puppy is slumped dead on the floor. He opens his eyes and catches sight of the corpse through the bars of the cot.

"P-p-puppy?" he croaks out. "Puppy?" he repeats, but sees the life has long gone. The moonlight strikes the body and the boy bites back tears. Choked horror keeps him from screaming, as a crude rope is revealed trailing from the dog's neck. A dark patch of something is slowly drying next to a mangled leg. Its rib bones stick out at odd angles under the skin.

The boy shuts his eyes again, this time not wanting to remember.

"That damn mutt! I'll show it!"

Big boots stomping across the floor.

"Shut up, shut up! Shut up! Woman, I'll do what I like, I'll teach it to bark into all hours of the night!"

A horrible silence follows.

"There, what did I tell you?"

He breathes slowly, letting tears drip down his face. He must not make a noise, no! Or he'll end up like poor puppy. That's what the man said.

Who was he? Was, was he... Daddy?

BANG!!!

The door comes flying off its hinges and smashes against a wall. The boy gasps and pulls himself away, trying to make himself as small as he can.

"Don't let him see you." Someone had said to him once. "Stay small and safe, don't let him see you at night." He can remember the urgent tone, and his promise.

"Do you promise me? Michael! Promise you won't let him see you?"

"O-Okay Mummy."

"There's a good boy, yes Mummy's little angel, yes, yes, small and safe, small and safe. You stay like that and you'll be safe."

A black shadow looms over the cot, as a figure approaches through the doorway. It stumbles, clinging onto the frame for support. At the back of his mind, he can remember Mummy, it must have been Mummy who said to stay safe. He remembers her hugs, her soft jumpers and candied perfume. She took him to the park once. They watched the big kids on the swings, flying through the air like the birds that live high up in trees. He wanted a go, but he was too little, "No, not till you're just a little taller."

"But I am taller, taller than yesterday, see!"

Something moans.

It snaps its head downwards to a lump which trails along the ground beside it. Another moan, Mummy's moan.

"Shut up!" it yells fiercely and flings the lump into the wall. There is a terrible crunching sound. He can hear it panting, mumbling about something, inane ramblings. "Why don't she shut up? Shh, need quiet, can't think, can't think! Quiet girl! I can't think. Do I have to hit you?"

He lies utterly frozen in terror, it hurt Mummy! It really hurt Mummy, my Mummy, the one with squashy jumpers and perfume that tickles my nose and the one who reads me stories about ugly ducklings and pretty swans!

The shadow turns and begins to walk away, bumbling as it goes.

"M-mummy?" The boy calls out. "Please let her be OK."

An awful silence follows, the ramblings have stopped. It has heard.

"I thought I TOLD YOU TO SHUT UP!" It bounds back into the room, hurling a bottle at the cot.

"You just don't know when to quit, do you?" it says as it staggers over to the cot. The boy shrinks in fear. He's broken his promise, now he isn't safe! A massive hand grips him around the leg and yanks him out of the cot. But his other leg is trapped in the headboard. It is brutally ripped away, he screams in torment. The smell of that candied perfume is swirling around it, the smell of Mummy.

"I said shut up! Didn't you hear me? Shut up! Shut up! Shut up!"

It lifts the shattered bottle. "Yeah, I'LL SHUT YOU UP!"

The boy whimpers like the puppy, held upside down, blood dribbles down him.

It stops suddenly and looks at the boy, its face softens, then smiles.

Shrieks echo round the building as the jagged bottle end is plunged deep into the boy's soft flesh, twisted and wrenched out.

It drops the boy and walks out.

"Finally, quiet."

The girl reappears in her living room, but doesn't give a second glance outside to the tramp. But he is looking at her.

He longs to be there, in that house, warm and well fed. He longs for the warm little house with the small, gently pruned garden. He is envious. Instead the tramp gazes at the house behind him. It is a scrawny thing whose ragged curtains flutter against the muggy glass. He closes his eyes in his last moments. The world breaks away from him, and finally there is quiet.

GEORGINA ASCROFT is 14 and lives in Jarrow in South Tyneside. She began writing her first novel (a Star Wars *tribute) when she was ten. She hopes to go on to study either law or stage management as she is also part of a junior theatre group in South Shields. She is inspired by people and music.*

The Hole

Penny West

I call my attic 'The Hole'. Everything that enters there has little chance of escaping. The velvety darkness lures objects into its lair and they are lost forever. As I look around at the numerous items littering hidden corners, I wonder, are there feelings stored in this place of cobwebs? Thrown aside like a child's forgotten toy? Though the attic is as silent as the grave, I can almost hear the endless thoughts and memories of my life tossed into this tiny, dusty room at the top of the house.

I dig into the pile as deep as I can and decide to work upwards to the more recent items.

A broken rocking horse, some moth-eaten baby clothes, a mobile of butterflies with some missing. Feelings of shame and regret flutter off their wings and fly away into the darkness. And it started with such a sweet happiness...

It is a curious fact that in England, there is perhaps just one week of brilliant, perfect weather that everyone will worship constantly outside until the dreaded return of the common cloud. When living in the Lake District, that week turns to one day. One day of deliciously hot, sunny weather in which you can play out until the midges appear and still mum won't call you in.

It was that day. I was four years old and had just finished a most satisfying picnic and was debating whether to have a nap. Sunbeams danced through the blades of grass in the playgroup garden and somewhere far away, a bird was singing to the world. The floral aroma tickled my senses and I felt I could want for nothing more. And then I saw it.

Resting on a branch near me, its wings fluttering lazily, its colours blinding me as the sun illuminated every glistening feature, sat a red admiral butterfly. I had never seen one before and was amazed at its beauty. But I was cursed with the evil of toddler-dom: I had to touch it. I could not contain my excitement at the thought of its silky, luxurious wings. I began my chase.

It outwitted me as I clumsily moved after it, but finally it was within reach. My chubby fingers slowly stretched out, but suddenly it wasn't just my hand that was moving, my body was too and I tumbled forward slightly, but managed to correct myself. Oh unfortunate fate! My toes grazed the creature's wings and it fell to the floor, a broken spirit.

"It will never fly again!" I only wanted a look. It wasn't my fault.

"Look at it, the wing is torn right off!" It was so pretty. I've gone all blurry, my cheeks are wet.

"You nasty child, how could you be so cruel?" Scream, scream! Leave me alone. I want to go home! Sob, sob. I want my mum.

A rusty bicycle, a pile of ancient newspapers, an old schoolbook covered in grime. On closer inspection, it is a book from my primary school. Here is a memory that is as dusty as the book, but I cannot help feel the tremors of fear vibrating from the pencil marks and scuffed pages. The mathematics book is full of jerked numbers, caused by sudden bellowing and some of the pages are a little blurred, though I pretend that is due to time and not tears.

Maths used to be my favourite subject at school until Class 4, when we were told a new teacher would be coming to take us for maths. He was called Mr Crabtree and someone had the good idea of calling him Crabby. Yes, it would be a good laugh having a new teacher, we decided, so we eagerly awaited his arrival.

The day came and we sat down quietly for once, unsure what to expect. When he walked in, I was hit by many different observations at the same time. The bowl-shaped cut of his brown, straggly hair; the thick black-rimmed glasses; the deep red colour of his face. He was a tall man, with broad shoulders, but something other than his size seemed to fill the room.

"Times tables!" he barked and we all jumped.

"You! Stand up!" he roared at a boy in the front.

"Five times seven!" The seven times tables were tricky, he certainly wasn't beating about the bush. The boy answered correctly though and Crabby nodded sharply and searched around the room, his snake-like eyes never blinking once.

"You! Stand up!" Oh no, he was pointing at Clara. This was going to mean trouble.

"Eight times nine!" The shock, the cruelty! Everyone know the nine times tables were the worst. There was a deadly silence. Clara began stuttering sounds that were obviously not the right answer.

"Well?" he hissed slowly. She glanced about nervously, but no one could help her now. She would have to make a guess, despite the suffocating pressure.

"Seventy-five?" The class waited with baited breath.

"SEVENTY-FIVE? You are nine years old and you are telling me you don't know your nine times tables? How I wish flogging had not been done away with, then you might learn something."

His face had turned purple now and Clara was making small, sniffling noises. Crabby was staring at her menacingly, hands outstretched, as if he would like to flog her there and then, rules or no rules.

"Sit down," he growled slowly and marched to the front of the class where every eye was upon him.

"We are going to learn the times tables and we are going to learn them correctly. Infants are taught this, I might add, but it seems necessary. Everyone will go home and learn the ones through to the twelves and there will be a test tomorrow. Those who fail will suffer the darkest consequences."

That night I worked like I had never worked before. If he just asked me an easy one, I might get out of class alive.

The next day our morning lessons sprinted by and we were genuinely shocked when our teacher left and Crabby strode in.

"I hope we all revised last night. I will question every one of you to see if you have put any effort in. Life is not just fun and games: we are here to work and you will word hard. You!"

The dreaded finger was hurled in my direction.

"Stand and tell me the answer to seven times nine!" Seven times nine? I had studied for ages last night and I knew the answer. But every feeling of stress, fear and the sudden desire to be sick or burst into tears, or maybe both, locked the answer firmly in my head and I knew I had no chance.

"Come on, we're waiting girl!"

"Is it... sixty-three?" I winced, but he just nodded abruptly and moved on to his next victim and I collapsed in my chair, relieved from the worry.

I spent Class 4 living in terror of the daily maths lesson. He slowly but surely drained all of my confidence and enjoyment of maths away like the wringing of a wet sponge. To this day I hate mathematics and can barely do mental arithmetic without getting worked up and having to guess at the answer, even to really simple questions. And I owe all this to Crabby.

A mangled tyre, some chipped crockery, a folder containing all of my souvenirs from when I went to Spain many years ago. A plane ticket escapes from its prison and trembles to the ground. I get a headache just looking at it. I have never in my life broken a limb, suffered a nosebleed or even had a brace. In other words, experienced the usual things that happen to children. However, there was an eventful plane journey that helped make me partly normal at least.

Spain. The ideal holiday destination. Just two hours away and a tan is within my reach. But I have to get there first. Alive, preferably.

As I sit on the plane and dream about the sun, it's covered over by black, swirling, violent clouds. My head begins to pound, my limbs begin to quake and my insides begin to churn. Everything feels wrong and the nausea and throbbing increase to an unbearable crescendo.

I am horribly sick, many times. Objects fly and spin and then reach the inevitable – the long spiral downwards into the black abyss.

I begin to daydream again, though this time it flows through my head and uplifts me. I am an angel and I float carelessly towards the sky...

Is she alright? Is she breathing?

Black.

Oh she looks so fragile. I caught her as she fell.

Just black. Wait! Now black and red.

I thought she was going to be sick again, but she just fainted clean away. Is she ill?

Little dots dance in front of my eyes. I remember playing in my back garden. I can see it vividly. Then I'm on a white sandy beach, with palm trees and a crystal blue ocean. It's so peaceful.

She's been unconscious for such a long time. I'm terribly worried. Can we get her a doctor or something?

There are no clouds here, no violent storm. I could escape from everything and stay here forever. Then I hear the faint melody of a desperate flute.

We have to help her.

I know I must reach out to the flute. As the tune soars, I realise how silent and lonely it is. I need this music. I need my family.

Is there anything we can do? No? WHY?

I am suddenly aware of the floor. It is comfortable and I wonder why I didn't think of lying on it sooner. I groan and stir dazedly.

"She's awake!" my auntie shouts elatedly and hugs me tight. For some reason my legs are being held by this stranger and I don't know where I am. Then I learn the truth. I fainted.

A skipping rope, a dusty desk, a neon water pistol, cracked in several places. My mum bought it for me for passing my maths exam. I insisted I didn't want it, but she told me I deserved it. I remember how awkward I felt, reminded, and the rush of guilt hit me.

"What's that under your jacket, young lady?" I froze. Every muscle in my body stiffened and I knew I was done for.

I suppose, deep down, I had known I was going to get caught. They had stood around me, moving like a pack of wolves going in for the kill. And I had been the unfortunate victim. They began to chant "Do it! Do it!" with Ebony, the leader, chanting loudest of all. She enjoyed seeing others take risks. Dangerous risks. But there were too many of them; I couldn't resist. So

I opened the door.

It creaked deafeningly as I slowly entered the toyshop. The decaying smell of wooden shelves hit me and I choked, though I doubt the stench was the real reason. I edged forward, my trainers making squeaking noises as I took step after step, spoiling the silence that hung in the air.

Why was I here?

Stealing was wrong: I knew that. But it was the only way to get | into Ebony's gang. And I just had to get in. People immediately wanted to be your friend and no one ever forgot your name. You were someone in her gang.

But the pressure of failure taunted me. I was going to get caught, or Ebony would decide I wasn't cool enough to enter her gang even if I did complete the dare. Then, alone and ashamed, I would crawl into a murky cave and never show my face again. This was my only chance to impress her, to prove to the world that I really was somebody. I would steal just one item and gain everything.

My hands itched hungrily for the glorious bounty I yearned for, and my feet moved faster, spurring me on to the finish line.

I peered round the aisle, my movements quick and sharp like that of a rat. I turned back to look at the window. Five faces stared back at me, their eyes beady, shining, their mouths practically watering at the thought of the danger. I could feel their thoughts breathing down my neck, forcing me onwards. However it was Ebony that stood out. Her face showed her complete control. She knew she was responsible for this and she loved it. Her nails scratched at the glass, desperate to be closer to my quivering body so that she might feel the gut-wrenching nerves grinding inside me. She gave me a sly sneer. Just looking at her unnerved me, but I had to focus on the task. One tiny mistake and everything would be ruined, and I did not want to face the devastated pack outside.

I found my feet walking as casually as possible towards the shelf. Thoughts pounded against the sides of my head and I felt it would explode, the pressure was so immense.

Then I saw it.

It was beautiful. The Gutblaster 6000. It was the most powerful water gun ever invented. I quickened my pace.

I reached out to touch it. And as the cool smoothness of the wrapper made contact with my fingertips, I knew I just had to have it.

Looking around I saw no one, except the man behind the till, but he was no trouble. Old Man Riley was as blind as a bat, they told me. Got wounded in some war and hadn't come back the same. Couldn't even hear properly, let alone see. He only ran the store because his son knew how trusting he was and exploited him constantly so he wouldn't have to pay someone. Or so they told me. Anyway, I should have no problem, they'd said. No problem at all.

In a flash I had grabbed the box. It was large and like a dead weight, and only just fit inside my jacket. My nerves spurted through my body, snapping at my skin, as I realised how obvious it was. I pivoted around and going as fast as my feet would take me, I headed towards the door.

Outside the window, the others were silently cheering. Ebony gave me a slight nod and I knew I was in. No words could describe my emotions. I had done it; I was the triumphant one. Just a few more steps and I would be a new person. I would step out of my cocoon, blossom like a butterfly and fly away into the sunset without a care in the world. I would be respected. Liked. Needed. I didn't walk out of that shop. I flew.

But the fairytale ending suddenly transformed into a horror story. And I was the ill-fated victim. All of a sudden I stopped moving.

The expressions outside changed from pleasure to sheer horror. The hand on my shoulder pressed down hard, along with my conscience.

"What's that under your jacket, young lady?" I froze. Every muscle in my body stiffened and I knew I was done for. I spun around. Old Man Riley's firm gaze stared into me. I turned to the window for support. Reassurance. Anything.

But no one was there.

They were walking away. They had already forgotten me and were joking around and shrieking gossip. It was as if I was in another world. But it was Ebony who angered me most of all. She was in front, as always the lone wolf, shaking her head sadly, as if to say, "there goes another one". And I knew she was right.

As the gang turned the street corner, I was certain they were going to go look for someone else. Another idiot, who hoped that if they did something stupid and pleased the gang, they could change who they were. That they could become cooler, popular, better and fly away, a new person. What a fool I was. I suddenly couldn't take the musty smell of the toyshop or the heavy weight of the water gun. It mocked me, just as everything and everyone else seemed to. It wrenched down on my heart and tore it to shreds.

I began to cry sharp, salty tears that stung my cheeks. I wiped them away fiercely, embarrassed I had given in to them so easily. Just like the gang. I then made myself a resolution: I would never give in again. It was that simple. I didn't care how much work it would take. I had let them convince me I was worthless, that I needed them.

Friends are people you trust. They take time and effort to make, but it is worth it. I realised I didn't need to change or prove myself. I liked me, and other people would if I let them and was myself. Bullies don't have real friends and neither do false people. I was stronger than anyone in Ebony's gang, including her. Now I knew this, there was nothing stopping me.

I felt my misery float out of my body and fly away.

As I turned to face Old Man Riley, even though I had been caught, I knew I was incredibly lucky to have failed the dare.

Aged rugs and bits of carpet, some woodlice scurrying across the floor, my old sleeping bag, now damp and covered in dirt. I stare fondly at its happy, colourful diamond pattern and its trusty zip. I have had many good times in this old friend. Camping and sleepovers had always been brilliant. Wait! I tell a lie. There was one time I will not forget in a hurry, due to a sinister occurrence that happened. And it took place within these very walls.

We had waited for this day for weeks. Nail files were at hand; facemasks were at the ready; magazines were bulging in our bags. We had taken an oath not to go to sleep and we had sworn to eat all the junk food we could find. It was to be my sleepover and I just knew it was going to be great.

There were about five of us, including Sarah Lennon. She was a vital part in the scheme of things as she had the all-important items: the videos. There was an immense collection – comedy, romance, action. But no horror. I had insisted upon it, as I am really quite cowardly and didn't want to show myself up. She had also brought some music videos, including a few by Michael Jackson.

"There's this really good one," she told us later on in the evening. "You just have to see it!"

"OK," we grinned, intoxicated with sugar. At that point, I think we would have agreed to anything.

She pushed it in the video recorder and pressed play. Some catchy music began and we all started nodding our heads to the beat. I began dancing idiotically, which made everyone laugh. Then I froze.

The story so far had been about a boy and girl on a first date, and they had driven to a secluded spot. A graveyard, coincidentally. At night. A full moon appeared from behind the clouds and Michael Jackson suddenly stopped and began to metamorphosise. He grew long, sharp teeth and yellow slit eyes. The girl, of course, began to scream and tried to run. But he was much faster then she could ever be. And he was hungry.

I was transfixed as evil creatures emerged from the ground and began chasing her. I gave a silent gasp as she screamed and began to breathe short, jerky breaths as she sprinted over the empty roads. The others were noticeably uncomfortable, and Sarah Cullen was hiding her face in a pillow. Even Zara, who is not normally affected, was gulping.

It ended with the whole thing just being a dream and the girl walked off happily. But then Michael turned round to the camera and his eyes were yellow slits. It stayed on that shot and the credits rolled. I couldn't take my eyes off his and it chilled me to the bone.

Sarah L laughed and turned off the TV.

"That was fun, wasn't it? What do you want to do now?"

The others might have mumbled replies, but I was concentrating on the yellow eyes of the cabinet on my left, and the black shadow that lingered near the window on my right. I was surrounded.

"What's wrong with you, woman? You're all shaky. You weren't scared by that video, were you?"

"Me? Course not," I laughed weakly. The others looked around nervously.

"Oh for God's sake. You don't seriously think Michael Jackson is going to come down the chimney, do you?"

Sarah C gave a small cry and we edged away from the chimney.

"I just don't believe this!"

"Yeah, you lot are really thick." I tried to save the last bit of pride left in me.

"I'm going to put an end to this." Maybe I had fooled Sarah. It would be OK, we just had to do something to take our minds off it. We'd be fine. Yeah, I was really quite brave when you think about it. Sarah was dead impressed - I could tell.

"Watch out! Here it comes!" Sarah flung open the door and turned off the light. I screamed and we all hid in our sleeping bags. No one dared move except Sarah Lennon, who sighed, ashamed of us, and lay down and went to sleep.

She was the only one. The next day my protest that my scream was really a sneeze was not believed, needless to say. I vowed to break every Michael Jackson CD I come across.

A pile of unwanted videos, some garish Christmas decorations, one deflated balloon. It reads across in large, bold letters "2000!" and even though the millennium was gone, my memory of it will never be.

The air was hushed. Every country in the world had proclaimed this night's importance and nature respected that. There was a slight chill, but this only tickled the hairs on the back of my neck and made my stomach tingle with anticipation. The new millennium had already come, sorry to disappoint you, but I was still waiting.

Not for fun, we had already had that, with the oldest and the youngest people (my nana and me) and the oldest and youngest dogs (Susie and my dog Trixie) walking in at midnight, calling ourselves the year two thousand. We had been videoed and my dad, slightly drunk, had left a message of goodwill to the future generation, which had been very touching, and then fallen over a chair, which hadn't.

No, tonight at half past one, I was finally alone outside and I began to search desperately for the new millennium. It wasn't in America or Australia, with their speeches and gigantic parties in the streets. It wasn't in London, where the Queen had spent the evening in the Dome, holding hands and singing with Tony Blair. It wasn't in the fireworks that surrounded my auntie's house and created sounds and colours I hadn't known possible. And it wasn't in the cut grass-scented breeze that whistled through the trees and the balloon I grasped tightly. Where was the new millennium?

I desperately needed it. It would bring life, and all its chances and decisions: the most precious things in the universe. Could I handle these responsibilities, beautiful yet perilous? The path of life was built in stars, ever changing and tempting. What if I strayed from the path and couldn't return?

Then I heard the laughter coming from my relations inside and felt the quick, rhythmic beating of my heart. I realised that I wasn't looking for the millennium. But I did want to find some things: I wanted to know that I would have the satisfaction of pleasing those whose opinions mattered most. I had to hear that we, as a family, would always be together. I needed to know that I would be safe in the years to come, and although they couldn't promise it, I knew they would give their lives trying. They would never let me stray into the dark.

My family and friends, with their ever-shining light that guided me as I walked down the path of life, they had the reassurance I was looking for, not a date on the calendar. I was searching for their love.

And do you know what?

I found it.

I have reached the end of the pile. Memories cry out to me, to think of them before I close the attic door and they are lost forever. I try to tell them that this could never happen. Every future smile, laugh or tear is because of them: for the talents and the strengths they have shown me, and the lessons they have taught. Without my memories I wouldn't be who I am today. For I am a real person, with faults and regrets, hopes and dreams.

Even so, I don't want to leave them, but I know I must. For the whole point of memories is to appreciate the present, use it wisely and live it to the full, so that your future memories are just as significant as your past ones.

PENNY WEST is 15 and lives in Barrow in Furness in Cumbria. She has always had a passion for writing and telling stories and has filled many note books over the years with ideas and thoughts which now influence her work. Everything in her story is true except for "one memory". She thinks that the craft of writing "forces you to think about everything and improve everyday. It would be an amazing experience to live like that." She hopes to go to Oxford to study English and her favourite hobby is embarrassing her best friend, Sarah Cullen.

Seascale Pier

As part of the Millennial Celebrations, it was decided that Seascale Pier should be reconstructed by way of a lottery grant, available only if the pier was built according to Victorian specifications.

The Victorians built it,
Way back when,

It lasted quite a while.

But not long enough for some.

And so it was built,
History in mind, the celebration
Of what has been,

And gone.

It was built, as some things are,
For the sake of it.
Like building something
In order to say
"Look, here,
Look at this.
This is what we can achieve

Sometimes."

But then,
"Suck a toffee and pass"
Is good advice, human endeavour
Being somewhat
Confectional
At best.
Anything we try to do with a purpose
Just seems to hurt people.

Better off playing with barley sugar
Than matchsticks, better

A pier than a plug socket
In the head of a cat.

Well, at any rate,
It looks like a pier,
Much as I imagine that this looks like a sneer,
Although it's not a sneer, it's a smile,
It just looks like a sneer,
Sitting in this face.

The gate to Seascale Pier
Has been there a year
And the sea breezes
Have rusted it.
The carefully wrought '2000'
Looks a hundred years old already.

It doesn't look man made any more, it looks like
Some creation spewn out by the Sea,
Covered in seaweed and slime,
Weathered and worn.

The waves break on the beach, a sure sign
Of time, cycles and seasons,
Ages and aeons, a sure sign that
We won't be here forever,
However hard we try.

The pier stands,
Thrown from the sea,
The skeleton of human achievement
Struggling from the Sands.

Tom Fletcher

TOM FLETCHER is 18 and is currently studying at Bretton Hall in Wakefield, although he is originally from Newcastle. He is inspired by Salvador Dali, music, his friends, "being outside" and "being inside". His poem originated from a moment when he was "the only person on Seascale Beach".

A conversation

Joanne Shields

Hello.
hello.
Anything you'd like to say?
-
Are you sure?
-
You know why you're here don't you?
yes.
And you have nothing to say?
no.
No reason behind it?
of course.
And what was it?
-
-
-
Well?
well what?
You're being very difficult do you know that?
yes.
Why won't you open up?
ok. when i was two my mother died and my father abandoned me. i was cared for by wolves and tore meat from the bone. when i was young i came to a man village after a fight with a talking tiger called shere khan.
You're not being serious.
so.
I would like you to be.
so.
Can we talk like adults?
yes.
Good. Would you at least tell me why you did it?
I'm fifteen. do i need a reason?
Yes. And you said you had one.
i do.
Have you always been like this?
no. i used to talk.

Then what happened?
she happened.
Who – your stepmother?
why does everyone blame the step-parents. no, julie is fine. it's her that's the problem.
And who is her?
my mother.
Does she hit you?
ha, if only.
Then what?
-
-
-
-
-
-
-

the men. all the god damn men she brings home. friends she calls them. friends. not only is she a whore but she lies about it too. not that everyone doesn't know. talk of the whole school. sean's mam's a slapper. and i can't deny it. it's true. she's just a stupid junkie whore.
Junkie?
yeah. half the time she's too drugged up to know what's going on. forgets to charge them and they get it for free. no wonder she lives in that shithole.
You don't like where she lives?
i have to go there on weekends. stay while she has fifteen or twenty 'friends' over. i have to hear what's going on.
And you don't go out?
where to? the streets are full of junkies with knives thinking up reasons to kill each other.
And you've never taken drugs?
that's an insult to me. what do you mean by that? just because i have a whore for a mother, i could get them from her?
I didn't mean that. I'm sorry if I implied that.
that's fine.
Where were we?
i could get them from her if i wanted.
Get what?
drugs from her. she leaves them round the flat. dirty needles in the bathroom, pills all over the floor, drink in the cupboards.

Do you drink?
i used to.
What happened?
she happened.
You keep saying that. What did she do?
you mean apart from being a junkie and a prostitute who is so off her face she forgets to charge?
Yes, all that aside?
is that not enough?
Quite enough but I can tell something else is troubling you. What else does she do?
it's not what she does it's what she doesn't do.
And what is that?
she doesn't care. not about me, the flat, anything. she doesn't even care about herself.
And is that why you did it?
-
-

she just doesn't care. the only reason she lives is to shoot up and have sex. she doesn't care about her reputation. she doesn't care that she's a whore and everyone knows it. all she cares about is the needles that go into her arm. not her son. not her life just her stupid stinking sex with strangers so she can get high!
Calm down Sean. I know this must be upsetting for you, and you can talk about it, but please calm down a little.
-
-
-

Sean?
-
-
-

Sean?
what.
Are you all right?
fine.
Do you still want to talk?
sure. what about?
Your mother?
no.

Your father?
no.
Your stepmother?
no.
Then what?
are you married?
Is that relevant?
i had to talk. now you have to as well.
OK. That's fair. But we must carry on talking about the incident.
whatever.
OK. Yes I am married. I have two children, both girls, one nine the other six. The eldest is called Sophie, the youngest is Anne Marie. My wife is called Mary. We are very happy and hope to have a few more children. Is that enough?
no.
OK. I live in a semi-detached house in a nice area. I buy the *Daily Telegraph* and enjoy trying to complete the cryptic crossword though the times when I achieve this are few and far between. I enjoy playing tennis and swimming with my girls. I like to read and sit in the garden relaxing on my days off.
go on.
What else is there?
how did you meet your wife?
We met at a bus stop.
romantic.
It was raining and the bus was late. We stood there for ten minutes before we started chatting. When we did I found out she liked tennis too and reading and we shared a common interest in travelling. Are you satisfied?
you don't seem to enjoy talking about yourself.
I could say the same for you Sean. You've managed to get a piece of my life story out of me and all you've told me is your mother is a drug addict and sleeps around.
-
-
-
-
-
-
Are you going to tell me any more or am I going to have to guess why you attacked...

ok, alright, fine. i'll tell you about my traumatic life. she's the only problem in it. if she was dead everything would be fine. no one would laugh and point and i wouldn't have to live with knowing my mother was a whore. people wouldn't mind being friends with me because despite what you may think i do have a brain and drug addiction and prostitution do not run in the family. i'm not going to be off my face all the time and acting like something special when all she is is a stupid little whore who hasn't got enough brains to see that her son despises her. i couldn't be like that.
You despise her?
-
-
-
-

That's what you just said Sean. You said you despise her.
i do.
Why? I mean why do you despise her instead of pitying her. I mean she's an addict. Addiction is not through choice.
it is in her case. if she wanted to change she could at least try. i told her i'd sign her up to a clinic and all she did was laugh and tell me if she wanted to change she would have done it years ago.
Maybe she was trying to mask her true feelings?
no she wasn't. i could tell. it was in her eyes. she enjoys being out of her mind. she told me responsibility was never her thing and being a parent proved it.
What did she mean by that?
that she knows how bad a parent she is and she doesn't even care. that's what she meant and why i hate her.
So why him?
what do you mean?
Why did you attack Mr Hargreaves?
honestly?
Of course.
because instead of attacking me he attacked my mother.
When? Last night?
no, in school. because i called him pin prick he turned to me and said that's not what your mother said to me last night.
He actually said that?
to my face. in front of everyone.
And that's why you attacked him?

i don't know. i just went crazy. everything in front of my eyes just went black then green then purple like a bruise. i saw his smirking self righteous prissy little face and everyone was laughing and i just thought that's the last line about my mother i will ever take. that's the last time i will be ridiculed for what my junkie slag of a mother does.
Then what?
i just stood for a minute and the room was sort of swaying a little and i could see his gums, he was smiling that much.
Who, Mr Hargreaves?
yeah, i just looked at his gums and they were so red. and i thought i want to make the rest of his face that colour. i want to make him bleed for what my mother does. and i don't ever want him to speak about her again.
So what did you do?
i just sort of leapt out of my seat and grabbed him by the collar and flung him against the wall. i hit him again and again and again and again. and it was working i remember thinking. he was going red and he was crying and screaming for me to stop and i wouldn't. even though i knew it was wrong and i should stop i couldn't. he was why i was in so much pain, he was why i had no friends, he was the cause of all my problems and he had to be punished. i wasn't even thinking about anything as i hit him. just thank god his face was red. and it was everywhere. so much blood it was unbelievable. i didn't know that much could come out of your face. and his teeth were breaking under my fist as well. one got caught and stuck in my knuckle. can you see the mark? i stopped to pull it out but it was in deep and by the time i had pulled it out someone was dragging me away and all i saw was the body with a pool of blood where the head should be.
Are you sorry?
i don't know. i'm sorry someone had to die but i'm not sorry it was him.
Why not?
because he deserved it.
No one deserves to be beaten to death Sean.
nobody but him.
And why him?
because he represented everyone who ever insulted me or my family and he had to be made an example of.
And is that what you think you have done?
i'm not sure. they will talk about him at his funeral as if he were a hero and say it was an unprovoked attack but i will know the truth. and at the end when the service is over everyone will go to the wife or mother's house for

drinks and sandwiches and say, well, what can you expect from the boy? his mother is a junkie whore. and i can't deny it.

This is purely a work of fiction. None of the characters depicted are based on real people, living or dead.

JOANNE SHIELDS is 15 and lives in Newcastle upon Tyne. She began writing when she was five and says that she continues to write because she "needs to". She is inspired by interesting people and enjoys reading and the cinema. In the future she hopes to become an author.

A Relationship

His cold eyes look sometimes
When he's not thinking greater thoughts
He sees her with muscles and curves
And no apologies made
He wonders if it's safe to fall in love with a
Socialist
Who has muscles
And curves

When he watches her it's more than just a look. He puts something on her which she has to take. Has to bear with a body so painfully self-conscious it won't let her stop growing and won't let her hide. Her Dad's a socialist. She only ever tried to be good.

He doesn't tell his friends that she's a
Socialist
With muscles, as well as curves
Instead he says he has a
Girlfriend who's a vegetarian
Which is a lie.
And then it is forgotten
He returns to greater thoughts (they are his destiny)
Trans National Corporations, for example.
Or the ever-increasing price of
Fish.

Rebecca Jones

REBECCA JONES is 18 and lives in Keswick in Cumbria. She began writing at junior school and her poem was inspired by "a geography lesson about trans national corporations". She enjoys drama and sports and hopes to go to university to study English next year.

Ghost

Gary Irving

The crow weaved in and out of the clouds, leaving a criss-cross pattern in the air. The black gleam from the underneath of its wing glistened and bounced off Kevin's eyes.
This was no ordinary crow.
It was way too big.
Kevin ignored the revolting bird, and carried on walking towards his home.
The sandy bricks rubbed against his school bag.
The house towered over him and made him feel so small.

Kevin kicked off his shoes and dumped his bag next to the sofa. He pressed the 'Power' button on the remote control. There was nothing on the television except a wiggling grey line, which had a faint outline of a person. Kevin tapped the screen, the figure in the television began to mumble something but Kevin couldn't hear it. The lines began to fade, only to reveal a 30-year-old woman. Her wrists had been slit, and the blood was wet on her hands.
Suddenly a crow started pecking at the window.
Kevin turned around and the bird flew away.
When he turned back to the television the woman was gone. Kevin decided it was only a television programme but from the corner of his eye he saw that the cable from the television was not in the socket.
Kevin stumbled to get up and fell over the sofa. He ran out into his front garden. He backed up, keeping his eye on the television through the window.
The crow shrieked from the aerial on his house. It swooped down towards him and plunged its sharp beak into his right arm. Blood came pouring out and was all over Kevin and the possessed bird. The crimson red stained his uniform and the bird's black cloak. The bird stopped, still on top of Kevin, and froze. It wasn't moving, until it heard a strange noise. A loud ear-piercing noise that made the bird fly away.
Kevin was left lying on the hard, concrete ground, still bleeding profusely. His vision began to fade and he began to fall into a very deep sleep.

He didn't know where he was but he could hear a familiar voice talking. He closed his eyes and listened to the conversation.

"So, doctor, what happened to him?" said a man who sounded vaguely like his dad.

"David, your son was attacked by a bird. We had to give him a lot of blood. We also need to keep him in overnight for observations."

"Why could I not give Kevin any of my own blood?"

"You are not of the same blood type, more than likely he is not your son. I am sorry," said the doctor.

"What do you mean he's not my son, of course he is!" shouted David angrily, stepping back in disbelief. "There must be some mistake."

"No, I'm sorry," said the doctor, "the blood tests confirm he is not your son." After an uncomfortable silence, the doctor carried on. "If you feel alright I have only one more question – do you want me to contact his mother?"

"No doctor, my wife has been dead for almost a year now."

"Oh... I am so sorry." The doctor felt his heart skip a beat.

Kevin opened his mouth and spat out a talon.

"Dad, where am I?"

"You're in hospital, you're okay now, you were attacked by a bird," Dad said, trying to look happy. "I'll be back in a while. Will you be okay Kevin?"

"Yes," he said.

As his dad left the room he saw the woman he had seen on the television walk straight through his dad's body, and turn around. She gave him a very disgusted look. Her wrists were still bleeding, staining her arm up to her elbow. Kevin was cold, his spine shuddered and he felt like his body couldn't move.

The woman began to walk towards him. Words stuck in Kevin's throat. He couldn't shout for help. The woman sat on the chair in the corner. She was wearing a hospital jacket with a nametag on. The tag read "Sara Jo..." Kevin could not see the rest of the tag – it was covered in blood.

Kevin managed to get out some words: "What do you want?"

Sara howled, "Beware." Then she pointed towards a figure walking past the window. "David," she said. It was his dad. Just then all the wounds on her body split open and blood spurted out and showered on Kevin's eyes. He wiped away the mess from his face, and then looked at his hands. The blood disappeared and the woman was gone.

His dad walked in, gave Kevin a cup of orange juice and told him he had to go home but that he would be back in the morning. Kevin's face was white.

Kevin woke up in the middle of the night, needing the toilet. His small feet touched the chilly floor and he started to walk towards the bathroom.

In the toilet the cold mirrors steamed up from the heat off the warm water he used to wash his hands. Behind him he heard a creak from the door. As he turned he saw writing on the mirror. He froze. It read:

'Beware!'

He pressed his finger underneath it and wrote:

'Beware what?'

It took a while but a reply came:

'David!'

The mirror shattered and the pieces flew at him. Strangely, nothing hurt him, even though nearly every piece touched his face. When he looked back at the mirror it was whole again.

Kevin ran as fast as he could towards his bed.

Sara walked out of one of the toilets and followed Kevin slowly.

Kevin wrapped himself in the duvet and put on a lamp. He knew if he told anyone they wouldn't believe him. He felt a cold draught go through him. Slowly he began to drift off to sleep.

As Kevin opened his eyes, a blurry picture of his dad began to come into focus.

"C'mon..." he began to try and force the next word out, "son... We are going home."

The road zipped by and the trees looked like green dashes of paint at the side of the road. Then he saw the ghostly woman, pointing at his dad. "David", she mouthed.

What does she want? Is it my mother? He just didn't know.

As they pulled up to his driveway, he saw the crow on the roof. Its burning eyes pierced through him like a pair of daggers. The bird soared away.

His dad was on the sofa next to him, but he looked mad. His face was all tight and red.

Yet again the television was unplugged, but Kevin could see something on the screen. It was his dad and his mum.

"Can you see that?" he asked his dad.

"See what? Oh the television... no I broke it last night... you won't be able to get anything on that old thing."

"But I can..."

"Just sit and eat your tea, boy!"

He watched the television and saw his mum and his dad having an argument. His dad slapped her and she fell over, she hit her head on the corner of the table.

Kevin looked at the corner of the table he was eating off, blood appeared.

He moved his eyes back to the television. He saw his dad fill up the bath and put his mother in it. He slit her wrists. There was blood everywhere. Kevin worked out his dad was trying to make it look like a suicide. Sara appeared behind the television and howled, "Beware!"

His dad didn't move. Kevin was the only one who could see her.

His mum disappeared, where she had been there was a crow. Its eyes sent a shiver down Kevin's spine. It soared around the room and landed in front of him. Kevin stumbled to get up, slipping on some blood that had leaked on the floor from the corner of the table.

He turned towards his dad.

"You did it, didn't you? All this time, I thought she committed suicide, but no, you did it!"

"What are you talking about?"

"You know fine well what I am talking about… YOU DID IT!"

"What?"

"I saw it on the television, then mum appeared, then a crow landed right in front of me… why did you do it?"

"You must be having a reaction to the tablets, calm down!"

"No," Kevin grabbed his knife from his plate, "you killed her, didn't you? You did, didn't you?"

There was a long silence. Then his dad replied, "Yes… I did, I found out she was having an affair. She kept arguing, saying it was all my fault… but it wasn't… she had the affair; I didn't mean to… but I hit her. She hit her head on the table, I didn't want to go to prison so I made it…"

"… look like a suicide," Kevin continued, still holding up the knife.

"Yes… and I am sorry. So put the knife down!"

"Never," said Kevin reaching for the phone.

His dad leapt towards him: "Don't call the police."

He grabbed the phone and pushed Kevin back against the wall. The knife was pushed into Kevin's arm as a result of him hitting the wall. Kevin started to bleed again. "Give me the phone," he screamed.

"No… Now if I take you to hospital, you will tell them what has happened, so…" His dad grabbed Kevin by his bleeding arm and pulled him up the stairs.

He threw Kevin in the bath and pulled the knife out of his arm. He had a mad, raged look in his eyes.

"Please Dad… help me…"

He slashed the knife across Kevin's wrist, cutting open his flesh and more blood started to pour out. Kevin was dead in seconds.

David filled up the bath, put the tablets next to Kevin and went downstairs to clean up the blood on the walls and the floor.

He made sure that he had cleared up all of the blood and put the knife in the bath.

He grabbed the phone and dialled the ambulance and the police.

"My son has committed suicide... I live at 13 Elmfield Terrace." He put on a fake scream for help.

Some time later David was at home when he heard a window smash from in the kitchen. He stood up and ran in to see what it was. One of the French doors had been smashed; all the pieces lay on the floor.

"Who was that?" he screamed half in and half out of the door.

There was no answer.

Standing in front of him were two bloody figures. His wife and Kevin. Their bodies had become rotten and parts of them had fallen off.

David panicked and tried to get away but his trouser leg caught on a piece of glass.

The crow soared between the two spectres and David fell over. He lost his balance and hit the ground. A shard of glass stuck through his neck. He tried to scream for help but he couldn't.

Blood was everywhere; it stained his clothes and his body. After a while he started to spit blood out of his mouth.

The two spirits watched as David breathed his last breath.

GARY IRVING is 14 and lives in Newcastle upon Tyne. He has only been writing creatively for a year and this story developed from English course work. His work is inspired by Stephen King novels and in the future he hopes to "write a series of novels and become a well-known author as well as a doctor of some sort".

A Split

I gain an ignorant impression of a surprised lady.
A picture of polite perfection.
Her hand in mine, she says,
"Grip tight and hold, dare to be bold,
The crazy beauty and freakish feelings hurt me too"
I stayed, delayed, and remain with delight.

Short Toll

To fall apart you must be whole,
Yet wholeness is a virtue,
A virtue held within you,
Within your cracking shell.

Thom Hurst

THOM HURST is 18 and lives in Wallsend, Tyne and Wear. He reads a lot and writes songs and plays guitar with a band. He is inspired by "people close to me despite distance and anyone with true love for what they do". He sees himself "in the melting pot of semi-talented musicians and writers striving to make it. Hopefully I'll be one of the successful few, if not I'll probably end up working forever away in a café".

Ghost Girl

Lisa Maughan

The fire crackled softly in the hearth, casting a warm glow over Hannah Thatcher. She worked carefully on a patchwork quilt, humming gently under her breath. Her youngest daughter Ellen lay asleep in the bed upstairs, curled up by the cat, Tabby, who purred drowsily by her side.

Her older daughter Sarah sat on the ledge by the upstairs window, looking out over the Derbyshire hills. She had a thick leather-bound book on her lap, her diary, which she was writing in.

16th April 1659
I am very worried about the situation that has befallen our humble village. A witch finder has arrived, and is causing havoc and fear amongst our innocent neighbours. Already this week he has hanged Goody Hall and Jemima Knight, both of whom I knew well. It is of the deepest misunderstanding that has caused Thomas Cornwell (the witch finder) to hang innocent women, and I hope that he will be stopped. I fear for the life of anyone who has an enemy, for they might find themselves accused of witchcraft! Oh how...

The silence downstairs was shattered by a loud thumping on the front door. Sarah stopped writing and looked out of the window, only to see a cluster of tall back hats. She couldn't see their faces from where she was sitting and she was curious to know who they were. She quickly jumped off the window ledge and crouched down onto the floor of the bedroom. She lifted up one of the planks and placed her diary in the cavity inside it. Then she removed a single ring from her finger and placed that on top of the diary. "Just in case," she thought. She replaced the plank and made her way downstairs to see what was happening.

Sarah was halfway down when she heard her mother's voice filled with fear.

"No, please! Do not take her! Please..."

"Mother?" Sarah said, stepping down.

Her mother looked anxiously over to her, and shook her head worriedly "No, Sarah, go back upstairs..." But it was too late. The men that had been standing behind Thomas Cornwell surrounded Sarah and grabbed her arms. Cornwell smiled menacingly and he watched Sarah's pretty face fill with terror as he spoke. "Sarah Thatcher, I have reason to believe that you have been practising the evil art of witchcraft. You must come to be proven guilty immediately."

Sarah was too shocked to speak. As the men led her away, her mother's shrill cries pierced through her thoughts, and she knew that the sound would haunt her forever.

Katie peered out of the window as her parents' car pulled up on the grassy verge outside their new house. Katie Thatcher-Smith was fourteen years old and had just moved down to the village of Fenford with her family. Apparently, there was a long line of her family history tracing back to this place, so when they had decided to move there, everyone found it very exciting.

As Katie and her sister Maisie piled out of the car, a grey cloud blew over the sun, and in the distance some thunder growled across the sky. "Oh great," Katie said aloud. "Our first minute here and already it's raining." Large raindrops began to fall faster and faster as she finished speaking, so within a few seconds, it was pouring.

"Come on, kids! We'll unpack later, but first we'll explore!" Katie's dad made the best of the situation and unlocked the front door. Everyone rushed into the house.

It was an original farmhouse, dating back to the mid 1600s. It was amazingly old, but had been built well so only needed a bit of renovation. There had been a new staircase installed behind the kitchen, the original fireplace was still intact and the downstairs ceiling had been reinforced with heavy oak beams. Everyone loved it.

The upstairs had once been a single room, but had since been converted into three smaller ones. Katie had rushed upstairs to choose a bedroom, and had found the one she wanted straight away. It was a smallish one with a window that had a ledge on it, the perfect place to sit. Katie climbed up and sat, looking out at the view of the rolling grey hills, stretching far into the distance.

The men led Sarah to a cart that was waiting outside her house. Sarah was tied to a pole at the front by her hands, and was humiliated by being made to stand in the cart as it was dragged by the men through the village. By the time they reached the 'ducking' pond, a crowd had gathered behind it. Sarah was untied from the pole and tied up again, though this time in the most peculiar way. Her left thumb was tied to her right big toe and vice versa, so she was in a tight, awkward position. Sarah's mother rushed up beside her and sobbed, "Sarah, I love you..."

Sarah didn't hear much more, as she was thrown into the pond by two sturdy witch finders. As a reflex, Sarah took a large gulp of air, so when she hit the water, she didn't sink immediately. Through the roaring in her ears, Sarah could make out voices.

"She floats! Guilty, she is! A witch!" Sarah was face down in the water and her lungs had begun to burn. "Will I die like this?" she thought. Suddenly, a pole pushed her violently toward the bank, and her face was exposed into air once more. As she was fished out of the pond, the crowd was silent. Sarah lay gasping on the bank, drenched to the skin and shivering.

As Sarah opened her eyes, a man stepped up to her. It was Thomas Cornwell. His voice echoed about her dizzy head, only sinking in seconds later. "You, Sarah Thatcher, are found guilty in the eyes of God as a witch. You shall be hanged at dawn tomorrow. May God have mercy on your soul."

A moment later, Sarah began to scream.

Katie was up bright and early on the first proper day in her new home. She dressed and breakfasted quickly, then called out to her mum that she was going for a look around the village.

"Okay, Katie, but turn your mobile on in case I need to ring you." Her mum reminded her, not looking up from her newspaper.

Katie strolled out over the grass front lawn in front of the farmhouse, switching on her Nokia mobile on as she went. The grass was soaked after the rain, and Katie had to walk carefully in case she slipped. She dropped her phone into her jeans pocket and began to hum as she walked through the main path through the village. She walked through the square where the market was being set up by a few yawning villagers. A friendly looking old man said hello to her as he unloaded his fruit from crates. 'What a friendly village', Katie thought, as she left the square and joined a little path that wound its way up to a small woodland area.

As Katie got closer to the trees, she noticed that just in front of it was a pond, covered in thick, green algae. She stopped as she felt a strange coldness wash over her. 'Odd' was the word that sprang to mind.

Katie leant over to look into it. "Huh?" Katie murmured, as a ripple passed over the spot that she was staring at. The ripple continued, even though there was nothing to cause it. Suddenly Katie saw a face in the algae. Deep beneath the water was a screaming, distorted face of a young girl, crying out silently. Katie yelled in surprise, then fell back, not noticing as her mobile slipped out of her pocket. She scrambled to her feet hurriedly, and ran back to her house as fast as she could.

The light was dim and tinged with pink, a beautiful morning on a tragic day. Sarah stood before the gallows, her hands tied with rope, so tightly that it hurt and made tears dribble down her cheeks. She had been screaming hysterically before, but now she felt oddly silent. She hadn't done anything, and yet she was being punished with her life. She was only sixteen, but she had been accused as a witch and ducked in the pond. They had said that someone had seen her in the woods alone, and Sarah couldn't understand it. She was not a witch; she knew she was innocent. But because she had floated in the pond, she was somehow a witch, and witches were hung.

Hung.

Hung.

Sarah was terrified, and she noticed a crowd slowly milling around the gallows.

Eventually, Sarah was tapped on the shoulder, and the executioner took her by the arm to lead her up onto the gallows.

Thomas Cornwell's face appeared at the front of the crowd, and he began to speak.

"This girl, Sarah Thatcher, was seen in the woods near our village - alone. We have significant reason to suggest that she was practising the evil art of witchcraft!" The crowd behind him gasped in disbelief.

"No!" Sarah whispered.

"The only suitable way to rid our world of such evil," Thomas Cornwell called, ignoring Sarah's protest, "is to execute Satan's followers! This Thatcher girl must die!"

"No! No! No!" Sarah's voice began to raise and get shrill, she was screaming for mercy now. "I am innocent! I am not a witch!" She was lifted onto a barrel, and she screamed as the noose was draped over her neck. "I'll never let you forget this! You are murderers and you shall go to hell!" Her words were directed at the witch finders, the accusers, the executioner, but most of all, Thomas Cornwell. A moment before her death, she looked up and found her mother's eyes in the crowd. She held them for a moment, whispered, "I love you" and then she was gone. But not forever.

"One story goes that over three hundred years ago, a young girl was wrongly accused of being a witch, and hung. She was said to have cursed moments before her death, that the people who had done that to her would never forget it, and that they would go to hell." Old Tom Greene spoke hoarsely, every now and then taking a drag from his cigarette and blowing it out slowly through his nose.

Katie had got talking to Tom Greene, the man who had said hello to her on her first day. She had asked him if the village was haunted, and because he was the village's oldest member, he might remember being told something.

"Anyway," he continued, "the witch finder went mad a few days later, and never accused another person of witchcraft. He was said to have repeated the girl's name over and over again until he mysteriously died. I think he drowned in the very ducking pond that he tested all the accused witches in. You know, if they sunk they were innocent." Tom took another drag on his cigarette. "If they floated they were guilty."

"That was such an unfair way to be judged," said Katie quietly, remembering the screaming face.

Tom nodded slowly, scratching his chin. "Yeah... I heard the old fool scratched his eyes out too. That's what your conscience does to you."

Katie thought about what she had seen the previous day. She hadn't told anybody about it, she was too afraid.

When Katie got home late that afternoon, her mum greeted her at the door. "Where have you been? I rang you on your mobile but you never answered. I told you to keep it with you, didn't I?"

"Yeah, I have it right here..." Katie stopped as she felt around in her pocket. "I thought I had it with me."

"You better not have lost that thing. Where did you have it last?" Katie's mum put her hands on her hips and sighed.

"Well, after you told me to turn it on yesterday I had it."

"And where exactly did you go yesterday?" her mum pressed on, jogging Katie's memory.

"Oh! I must have dropped it by the pond!"

"What pond? Just go and get it then come back straight away because your tea will be ready." Her mum began to turn back into the house.

"But mum, it's getting dark and I don't want to go on my own." Katie accidentally spoke in a whiney voice, and immediately realised how babyish she sounded. But she couldn't tell her mum what she'd seen. After all, she'd only think it was an excuse. "I'm going, I'm going. I'll be a few minutes," Katie sighed and began to jog across the lawn to the path. "I'd better be quick; I really don't want to be near that pond when it gets dark."

As soon as the pond came into view, Katie felt the same chilling feeling all over her. She froze, her eyes darting about quickly. "Just find the phone, and run home," Katie reassured herself, and took a deep breath.

She quickly made her way over to the pond, and looked around where she thought she'd been the other day. She couldn't see it anywhere. At last, she spotted it, except it was way over the other side, on the side nearest the trees. "How on earth...?" Katie murmured, walking carefully around the perimeter of the pond. "I wasn't over here!" She picked up her phone and slipped it fully into her pocket, then turned to go back.

Suddenly, she saw something that made her stop and stare with horror. A figure of a man was sitting on the bank of the pond, his feet immersed in the water. He wore a long black cape, old-fashioned style, and a tall black hat. She didn't see his face until he looked up. He was quite old with long grey hair that fell past his ears from under his hat. He had a thin grey Stuart moustache. But it wasn't the fact that he was murmuring "Sarah Thatcher, Sarah Thatcher, Sarah Thatcher" over and over again that made Katie call out. It was his eyes. Or the fact that he didn't have any eyes at all. When he turned to look at Katie, she saw that where his eyes should have been, there were deep black holes. Bloody and torn, his sockets were gazing blindly at her, sinister and evil.

Katie screamed and ran into the woods. She could hear the man calling eerily, "You were right, Sarah Thatcher. Why are you running? You were right!"

Katie ran into the woods for what seemed like ages. The woodland looked small from the outside, but as she was running she seemed to pass hundreds of trees. Katie ran until she was too exhausted to run any further. She stopped and turned around, but only saw rows of trees, holding darkness between them like a net. There was no man or ghost following her. It was getting dark fast, and she was all alone. Katie began to cry, terrified.

From somewhere to her right, she sensed a movement between the trees. "Hello?" Katie said, getting ready to run again if need be. She peered into the trees to her right, and saw a pretty young girl's face peep out from behind one. The girl walked slowly out from behind the tree and came into view.

Somehow, Katie knew this was a ghost too. Except Katie wasn't as afraid of this ghost, for obvious reasons.

It was a girl, about 16, who wore a long pale grey dress, a white apron and shiny black boots. Curls of blonde hair fell out from under a soft white cap – she looked like she was from the distant past. Her face, however, was pale and withdrawn; she had dull blue eyes and she wore an expression of immense sadness.

Katie plucked up the courage to speak. "Hello. Who are you?"

The ghost blinked in surprise, before speaking in a very quiet, far-off voice.

"My name is Sarah Thatcher. Who might you be?"

"I-I'm Katie Thatcher-Smith," replied Katie, feeling less uncomfortable than she knew she should be.

The ghost's face showed an expression of astonishment. "We must be related..." she whispered thoughtfully, drawing her eyes away from Katie and looking behind the spot where she stood.

She sighed heavily, and then looked at Katie again. "You saw that man back there, didn't you?"

"You mean the other ghost?" Katie asked.

"The man by the pond. His name is Thomas Cornwell."

"He frightened me," Katie responded.

The ghost nodded. "He once frightened me, too. But not anymore – he's just a mad spirit now."

"What do you mean?" Katie was puzzled, but the ghost carried on speaking in her quiet tone.

"He did something unforgivable a long time ago. I almost wish I'd been a real witch and then my meaningless curse would really have worked. But it all happened so long ago... I just want to leave now. You met me for a reason and I was wondering if you could get something for me."

Katie was weary and confused, but the girl seemed deadly serious and obviously needed this thing, whatever it was. "Okay," Katie said. "What is it?"

"My diary. It's in my room. I need someone to discover the truth." Then Sarah vanished into the darkness between the trees.

Katie wasn't sure how she got home that night, she just vaguely remembered walking back through some trees and then knocking on her door. She didn't know whether she'd walked past the man by the pond or not, or if her mum scolded her for being late, or whether she even knew where to look for Sarah's diary. She simply trudged upstairs and fell into bed.

Katie woke up the next morning, and remembered everything. She felt oddly calm, however, as if she understood parts of what had happened. The mist had settled after the night before, so when she got up to look out of the window, she could only see greyness and the faint blurs of far off trees. She opened her wardrobe and put on her favourite dungarees and pale yellow t-shirt. She opened the chest of drawers by her bed and found the box with her earrings in it. She took it over to the window ledge and placed it down while she opened it. Sarah picked up her favourite stud, a small silver cat's head, and admired it, twirling it round in her fingers.

"Katie!" Her mum's voice startled her, making her jump and drop the earring. "Breakfast!"

"Oh, no!" Katie sighed. She crouched to the floor and began feeling around for her precious earring. The floor was only plain planks of wood, though they had obviously been varnished many times. Katie's fingers closed around her earring, and she silently breathed a sigh of relief. She was just about to get up when she paused, her fingers feeling a small notch chipped out of the edge of a floorboard, almost like a handle. She slid her fingers under it, and pulled. She had to tug quite hard to dislodge the layers of varnish that had collected around the plank's rim, but it must have been very loose to start with, as it came up completely.

Katie put the plank aside and peered into the space under the floor. She reached down and carefully lifted out a thick, leather-bound book. As she did so, she heard a quiet clink, and put her hand down again to find what had caused the noise. Her hand closed around a small silver ring, with a tiny heart engraved on the outside band. "Wow," Katie mumbled, then sat back and opened the diary at a random page. As soon as she started reading, she realised that this was Sarah's diary.

3rd April 1659
I met Oliver in the woods again today. I know it seems suspicious but he's Thomas Cornwell's son, and old Corny won't be wanting me to see his son. Thomas Cornwell is the witch finder, you know, the one who is hanging people he thinks are witches. On a brighter note, Oliver gave me a silver ring, and he carved a heart on it himself. It's beautiful, my pride and joy. I'll keep it safe forever, and I promised him that. We are going to get married someday!

14th April 1659
I was walking in the woods with Oliver again. It's the only time we can be together without much fear of being seen. I am a bit worried though because I thought I saw someone spying on us. If anyone finds out that I am going to marry Oliver, then they will surely tell his father, who won't hear of it at all. I suppose he wants Oliver to marry some respectable lady, not an ordinary farmer's daughter like me. I haven't told my mother yet of my plans, but I will soon.

15th April 1659
I saw Thomas Cornwell today, from across the church hall. He gave me the most awful look – I dare not even wonder what he knows about me. I hope he doesn't know about Oliver and I, I do not trust him and I can't imagine what he's capable of. Oliver has mentioned before that he goes to the most extraordinary lengths to get his own way...

Katie snapped the diary shut. She slowed the thoughts wildly whizzing round her head, and gradually, they began to make sense.

Katie went to the woods again that night. She knew Sarah would find her, and sure enough, a few minutes after Katie arrived, Sarah appeared.

"Katie, did you find my diary?" Sarah walked toward Katie, her sad face looked expectant.

"Yes. I think I know what happened, but could you explain it?" Katie clutched the diary, unsure whether to give it to Sarah or not.

"Very well," Sarah smiled sadly. "I was in love with Thomas Cornwell's son, Oliver. I knew that Thomas would never let me, an ordinary farmer's daughter, marry his son. Oliver and I planned to get married, but... we never could." Katie thought she saw Sarah wipe a tear from her eye. "I was accused of being a witch by Thomas Cornwell but they didn't have proof. I wasn't a witch, but they they killed me. I died, and I know something wasn't right about it." She looked down sadly. "That's why I'm still here."

"Yes..." Katie wondered, the pieces of the puzzle fitting accordingly. "Thomas Cornwell found out about you and Oliver and accused you, because he didn't want his son to marry you. He used witchcraft as his excuse."

"I think," Katie continued, "I think Cornwell went mad after he killed you. Even he had a conscience, and he couldn't handle it." Katie watched in amazement as a smile spread across Sarah's face.

"I knew it. I was wrongly accused and it was all a plot devised by Cornwell to get his own way." Sarah's voice had brightened considerably.

Katie spoke again, determined to fully understand. "Oh, one more thing. Sarah, when I saw Thomas Cornwell by the pond the other day, he asked why I was running. He said I was right about something."

Sarah smiled again, as if finally getting a distant joke. "Yes. Well, before I died, I said he'd never forget what he'd done, I said he'd go to hell." Sarah shrugged. "He did go mad though, didn't he? I was right after all, my curse wasn't completely empty!"

Katie smiled too, remembering Tom Greene's words and glad that this poor ghost understood everything at last. She suddenly remembered what she was clutching in her hand and lifted it towards Sarah.

"I also found this." Katie held out the silver ring. Sarah's face lit up and she held her hands out for it. Katie placed it on the ghost girl's pale fingers, and watched, amazed, as Sarah slipped the ring on as if she were alive and solid again. Sarah looked up at Katie and spoke softly.

"I went to my grave without ever really knowing what had happened. I was so restless and couldn't remain in peace. Now I am quite content now that you, Katie, a distant relation of mine, know the truth and can see the whole story. You've helped me be free again." She leaned over and gave Katie a cold peck on the cheek. "Thank you," she whispered softly in her ear.

Sarah began to walk away, but she stopped after a few paces before turning round once more. She winked cheekily, smiled, and said, "Oh, and don't worry about seeing Old Corny again. I was right, remember? He's going to hell!"

With that, the ghost girl walked off into the woods, laughing softly to herself.

LISA MAUGHAN is 14 and lives in Newcastle upon Tyne. She has been writing stories since she was five and enjoys the work of fellow authors JK Rowling, Arthur Golding and Jacqueline Wilson. Her story was inspired by the book Witch Child *by Celia Rees and the film* The Crucible. *In the future she would like to pursue a career in the field of art and design and to "write books in her spare time".*

Spider

Legs of eight, eyes of many,
Spinning in the air lacey iron.
Winged creatures entombed.
Phobia. Fright.
Black as a night sky
Without a moon.

Peter Morgan

PETER MORGAN is 14 and lives in Ellington in Northumberland. He started writing when he was six and is inspired by natural history and observation. He enjoys cycling and fishing and would like to write more in the future.

Esther Wood

Hope Whitmore

Esther walks into the careers room. This is the first time she has seen a careers teacher. He sits there at his desk with his bald head shining in the light. Esther notices that his desk is terribly tidy. There are a few pieces of paper that are all stacked neatly in piles and on each side of the room there is a bookcase, each shelf labelled alphabetically.

"Take a seat," he says.

Esther notices he is smiling patronisingly as he says this but she obeys.

"And you are Esther Wood, I suppose?" he says.

Esther nods.

"Good," he says. "Now let's have a look at your SATs results, shall we?" He opens his desk and after a moment of searching he pulls out a file. "I see you got a level four and two level threes," he says.

Esther nods again.

"And do you have any ideas what you'd like to be when you grow up?" he says. She knows he expects her to say no or shake her head because she seems to him the kind of person who'd do that.

"Yes," she says. "I want to do environmental science."

"Well," he says, taken aback. "Do you know what environmental science will involve?" She knows again he expects her to say no. Again he is taken aback when she says yes, she does know something about what doing environmental science involves and she knows about university.

"You do understand," he says, "that you have to pass examinations to go to university?"

"Of course I understand," says Esther. She doesn't add, "Do you think I'm a moron or something?" She feels she has to keep remarks like that to herself.

"And you think you'll be able to pass these exams, do you, Esther?" he asks.

"If I work hard enough, yes."

"But in your SATs you didn't get a good mark for science. That means you probably won't pass other exams like GCSEs next year."

"I can try to do better then," she says.

"Yes," he says. "I suppose you can improve your science result a little, but your SATs really should be a pointer to what you're good at."

"So you mean I'm good at nothing," says Esther.

"I'm not implying that at all," he says. "I just think you ought to think about something you'd be good at, such as a shop assistant perhaps, where you wouldn't have to be so intell... I mean, which wouldn't be so academically demanding."

A picture of a woman handing over a bag of sprouts and giving change pops into her mind. She pulls a face and shakes her head. Then she decides that this ant-feminist statement needs more rebuking. "You know," she says, "You're right about SATs. They should be a pointer, they should point out how much harder I'll have to work to get to study environmental science, but whatever you or anyone else like you says, I am going to stick to my ambitions."

Just then the bells goes and both Esther and Mr Gibson breathe a sigh of relief and Esther leaves the room.

Esther walks out onto the crowded tennis court. She heads purposely for the quietest corner, hoping she won't be noticed. Unfortunately, within a matter of minutes, someone has noticed her. Lara Payton, Stephanie Hurst and Freda Ash, who have become bored with their attempts at a game of tennis, saunter over. They are in the same year as Esther but in all the higher groups. Also, they're pretty, but the factor that makes them most powerful is that they have each other and Esther has no one.

"Hello, Esther," says Freda.

Esther ignores them. She knows what will come next and she tries to avoid it.

"Hey," says Lara. "Freda said hello."

"Maybe she's gone deaf as well as being stupid this time," says Stephanie. Lara and Freda giggle.

"I'm not deaf and I'm not stupid," shouts Esther feebly.

"Oh, she's talking now," sneers Lara.

"So," says Stephanie, "how did the careers session go?"

"Did he tell you you're stupid?" says Lara.

"He probably did," says Freda. "He tells the truth about everything. He said I would be a great chef."

All the people you cook for will get food poisoning, thinks Esther, but she doesn't say it.

She turns and starts walking away but they follow her. Eventually she plucks up the courage to turn round and face them. "Well?" she enquires. "What do you want?"

"We just want you to know you're stupid," says Lara spitefully. "Very stupid."

That night Esther clambers over the rocks to her little bit of beach, the bit nobody ever comes to because it's too hard to climb to over the rocks, the bit of beach she's been coming to since she discovered it four years ago.

At first it was a place of adventure but in the last few months it's become a place of retreat, a place to be alone except for the sea. She likes the sound of the sea and the waves. Esther sits on a big stone and watches the sea. She takes off her shoes and digs her feet into the sand. She feels slightly soothed by the cold powdery sensation. She thinks about the events of the day and her nose begins to hurt. Her eyes well up with tears. She looks up at the sun, it looks as though it's got a rainbow round it. Esther smiles. Whenever she cries a rainbow appears around the sun. A magic rainbow that no none else can see. It's the sun's way of cheering her up.

On the beach Esther sees a worm. Poor thing, she thinks, its whole body is encrusted in sand. It's all dried up. Next to the worm is a shell, one of those razor shells. Esther puts the shell in her rucksack before heading towards home.

When she gets home Esther puts the shell on her window sill along with her other shells and fossils. She picks up one of the ammonites and stares at it. She holds it in her hand, thinking how old it is before placing it carefully back next to the photograph of a boy who is perhaps her father, she doesn't know. All she knows is that she was born when her mother was sixteen and her father left, unable to cope. Mum says the photograph is of a friend but Esther believes he is the man she should be able to call Dad.

She picks up the razor shell again. She thinks about her bad SATs results. She thinks about her visit to the careers teacher. She thinks about Stephanie and Lara and Freda and about the father who hated her so much that he left.

What if I am thick? she thinks with despair. What if I can't get anywhere? She pulls up her cardigan sleeves and runs the razor shell down her arms. She sees trails of blood and feels she's won a great victory. She does it again and again and again. The satisfaction is overwhelming. She continues cutting her arm until she realises Mum will soon be in from work. She runs to the bathroom and washes the blood from her arms in a panic.

After she's washed she goes to her bedroom and selects a long sleeved cardigan that will hide her scratches.

"So how was school today?" asks Mum.

"Fine thanks," murmurs Esther. She stares at her plate of cottage pie. Usually Esther likes eating but tonight she sees the meal as a challenge. She can't stop thinking about what she did earlier. All the satisfaction she felt before has been replaced with guilt and bitterness. She wants to tell her mum everything but she doesn't. She knows Mum would be shocked and hurt if she found out. and she makes a promise to herself that Mum will never find out.

"So, any questions, class?" the maths teacher, Mr Morston, asks. Mr Morston is a middle aged man, the only middle-aged man Esther knows who doesn't wear glasses, and he is surprisingly tall, about six foot five. Esther sticks up her hand.
  "Yes, Esther?" he says.
  "Is there such a thing as a left angle?" asks Esther.
  The class giggle.
  "No, Esther," says Mr Morston. "There is no such thing as a left angle."
  Now everyone is looking at her. Esther feels really stupid and she folds her arms on the desk and puts her head down.

Esther sits in the canteen with a slice of pizza and a doughnut. Lara, Freda and Stephanie notice her. They deliberately head for the table Esther is sitting at.
  "You should be more careful what you eat," says Freda.
  "Yeah," says Lara, "you don't want to get fat, then you'd be uglier than you already are."
  "Is it possible for her to get uglier?" says Stephanie.
  "Well, it's definitely not possible for her to get stupider," sniggers Freda.
  They look at Esther and laugh.
  Esther gets up and puts the remains of her pizza in the food trash. What a waste, she thinks. She would have liked to have finished the pizza but she can't because of these three people.

Esther walks in from school that night feeling pretty foul again. I am stupid, she tells herself. She takes out a pen and paper and writes:

Reasons I am stupid
1. Even the teachers seem to think I'm stupid.
2. I got the worst marks in my class for SATs.
3. Why would Freda and Stephanie and Lara be so horrible if I wasn't stupid?
4. I haven't noticed my stupidity until now, possibly because I was too stupid to notice it.
5. Lara, Stephanie and Freda are the cleverest people in the class so they should know what they're on about.

She picks up the list and puts it neatly under the carpet before setting off to her special place. The tide's right in when she arrives. She sits just in front of the sea. Then all of a sudden she has a strange urge. She throws off all her clothes and runs forward, putting all her effort and concentration into what she's doing, yet not thinking of anything except freedom. The sea is freezing but she doesn't feel it. She runs forward and when she's beyond her depth she swims forward and away from the land until she feels herself losing energy. She looks behind her to check that she can't see the land any more and when she's satisfied with her distance from all she's left behind she lets go and lets herself become part of that complicated mass of time known as the past.

HOPE WHITMORE is 17 and lives in Kirkby Lonsdale in Cumbria. She started to write "when I was about five and my dad got his first computer. I used to go on it and write. It was like magic." Her story is based on personal experience and is inspired by fellow writers Sylvia Plath, Emily Brontë and Virginia Woolf. She enjoys debating contemporary issues, swimming and spending time with her dog Spring. In the future she wants "to be spontaneous".

Searching for Silence

She thought she heard silence once.
Thought she heard it, amongst the inconstant hum of the tacky plastic lights and broken
Buzz of the air conditioners,
Which droned on, relentless.
She thought she would hear it, when, somewhere within the school, a cup dropped,
And the clang of the hollow sound reverberated round for a minute, bouncing,
And then was gone.
She thought she could hear it invade, seeming suddenly loud and intimidating.
It eluded her, sharply.
Echoes of laughter floated up from the assembly hall, where rows of pupils sat,
Bored no longer, now watching, entranced, mimics of the teachers.
New additions to the noisy, ever-present silence.
No silence there.
Footsteps.
Sudden, in the stillness.
Their sound echoed, like the soft, simultaneous beat of a drum and clash of a cymbal.
Sharp taps, with strangely different resounding echoes.
A door creaked open.
A teenager.
No silence there.
None, except in the wordless questioning look round, searching.
Then she was gone.
Her footsteps retreated down the corridor, clacking;
Tall heels piercing the darkness and then receding.
A door whined open and then closed, wavering on the edge of darkness.
Then a quiet thud as it joined with its counter-part.
United.
Once again, that near-silence.
Imminent, and yet still evasive.
She was hovering on the verge of catching it.
Deep down below,
Somewhere within the network of corridors where she looked for silence,

Another door opened.
A different door, unmasking different secrets.
Secrets no longer.
A flood.
Of laughter, noise; deep contrast to the quiet hum of mechanical friends.
A spillage of people in different directions. Seeping.
The effervescence travelled, a mounting cacophony,
And radiated upwards like the children, excitedly talking and discussing.
More doors opened.
Heavy footsteps and laughter
Suddenly, an implosion.
People bursting in, travelling in different directions.
They opened their bags, like the opening of cages,
And the last torn remnants of the defeated silence flitted upwards,
Avoiding any capture that the presence of humans could bring about.
Quietly, she slid off her desk,
And slipped inconspicuously into the busy bustle of school life.
It had escaped her, and she would not find it.

Helen Koelmans

HELEN KOELMANS is 15 and lives in Newcastle upon Tyne. She started writing a year ago when a story that she wrote about a moth came second in a wildlife writing competition. Her poem was inspired by a moment in time: "On Friday mornings I lead a horn quartet in another school instead of going to assembly. On this occasion it finished early so when I got back the classroom was empty and it was all so quiet. It was beautiful." She hopes to visit Africa in the future and to continue to be inspired by everyday things for, as she says, "life is too complex to just pass things by".

Drink

At first the splash of an idea ripples
amongst the imaginary, oscillating waves.
Distorting truth, but it seems order is there.
As the water level settles, usually
the meaning will sink like a rock,
but sometimes
the words form on the surface of
reality – mirroring society,
though transparent to the secrets
and truths of the depths,
urging the drinker to look closer.
Clarity in the crystal clear
words, like ice-cold water.

Neil Singh

NEIL SINGH is 17 and lives in Hartlepool. He has been writing for two years. His work comes from his "fascination with the complexity of the world". He canoes, plays guitar with Dave's brother's band and hopes to become a doctor. Alongside this he would like to create a book of poems about young people in the North East.

The Comfort of Fear

Dominic Freeston

They say that just before you die, your whole life flashes in front of your eyes. That night, standing at the bridge, I sincerely wished it were not true. My life was the very thing I was trying to escape. The idea of this being the last thing I was to see sickened me more than what I was about to do.

Hanging onto the edge of the bridge, I felt the wind whipping my face, while the sound of crashing waves down below filled my ears. I dared open my eyes for a moment and stared at the dark abyss just below my feet. As I looked I felt something gently tug me down. It was as if a presence were pulling me, telling me to join it wherever it was.

As I felt my grip loosening, I came back to my senses and held tight. Suddenly, I tried to remember why I was doing this. Two voices inside my head had started a heated debate. The first argued that it did not matter, and that it was too late to change my mind. My life was a living hell, the best thing to do was to escape from it. This was the only way. The other was trying to convince me that I did not really have a good reason to do this, and that I was simply being stupid. Unfortunately, emotion usually beats reason, and the first voice quickly drowned out the second one.

Just as I was about to jump, I heard an alien voice, something that should not have been there. It was incredibly high pitched, and something inside told me I should not be able to hear such a sound. It occurred to me that I might have jumped already and that this was what death was like. I looked around and felt the cold steel under my hands. I could still feel the wind and hear the waves not so far away. I was still hanging tight at the top of the bridge.

A faint light appeared below my feet. I looked into it, and instead of the river lying at the bottom, I saw a field. The grass was dark, and the few trees appearing here and there were of the same colour. What scared me was that I could not define the colour. Everything looked dead. A breeze caressed my face. It lacked the violence of the previous wind, but it filled me with fear. The stench of death was all around me.

Suddenly the voice I had heard before rose again, but I could hear it clearly this time. "Come to me. Come and see." No words ever evoked so much fear. I tried to scream, but no sound emerged from my gaping mouth. I held on to the rail behind me, but the 'thing' was pulling me down. I felt my arms weakening, I lost my grip, and then... darkness.

When I awoke, it took me a few minutes to realise where I was. My brain was pushing against the inside of my skull, wanting to explode. The pain was excruciating for a few seconds, but then it suddenly disappeared. I laid down on my back, trying to remember what happened. It slowly came back to me... I realised that it was grass under my neck, not my pillow. I sat up quickly, and I noticed the horrible darkness all around me. About two hundred metres away I could see one of the trees. Shivers went down my spine, but I was no longer scared. I looked up. The sky, if there was such a thing, was empty. There was no sun, nor stars... but I could see. There was no source of light visible, but somehow, I could see.

I stood up and looked around. There was nothing for miles. As far as I could see there were only dark and deadly plains. Strangely enough, I felt no fear. Once again, I considered the possibility that I might already be dead, and that I was condemned to roaming around this emptiness forevermore. I remained lost in my thoughts for what looked like an eternity, when suddenly, I heard another voice.

"Welcome to Hell, Outsider!" I looked around. There was no one. "Hell?" I asked. "Does this mean I'm dead?"

"I'm afraid not, Outsider, you are only visiting... against your will maybe, but still only a visitor. Look at me when I'm talking to you!"

I looked down and saw the strangest creature. It was about two feet tall. Trying to describe it is like trying to describe snow to someone who has lived all their life in the tropics. I can state its colour, which was dark green, and its texture, which was slimy and wrinkly, but I cannot describe the impression when you see it with your own eyes.

"What are you?"

"What am I? I sincerely hope you meant, who am I? My name is Spindgly, at your service. Please follow me."

It bowed clumsily in front of me, then started to walk towards... well towards absolutely nothing, for there was nothing to walk towards. I was too confused to argue, so I followed it, or him, because I was still not sure of who or what it was. We walked for a few minutes, or possibly a few days, and each time I tried to engage the thing in conversation or ask a question, the only reply I got was, "Outsider must not ask question, follow Spindgly, wait and see." So I did.

As we walked along, I saw a tall building appearing in front of us. Maybe the plain was not so empty after all. I realised that Hell did not obey the normal physical laws of the world and that because I couldn't see anything it did not necessarily mean nothing was there.

The creature that called itself Spindgly opened the door of the tall, dark building. It moved out of the way to let me in. I was expecting my legs to start shaking, or for my hands to sweat at any moment, but somehow, I still did not feel any fear.

"Why am I not scared?" I asked myself out loud. The answer came not from me, but from my strange companion:

"You mean fear? There is no place for emotion here. I never feel anything. I wonder what it's like... Love. I heard a lot about it..."

"Is that what death is about then?" I asked myself. "The loss of feelings..." I turned to Spindgly. "If this is Hell, does Heaven exist too?"

"I don't know," answered Spindgly. "People come here and they are assigned an occupation and they do it. That's all I know, that's all I need to know. I'm just here to guide people. That's my job, I guide people."

As we were speaking, I found myself entering the building. The door closed behind me, and all was dark. This time, I could not see anything. A weak glow appeared at my feet, and looking down, I saw Spindgly's head shining, but with a dark and gloomy light. He started to trot along, and I followed.

We walked for a completely timeless period through many corridors and many doors. The place was a complete maze. Eventually, we reached a door that was different to all the others. It was twice my height and five men could have gone through it at once. There was some form of writing on it, but I could not make out what it meant. It was beautiful, but repulsive at the same time.

The door opened of its own accord. I looked down at Spindgly, but found that he was gone. I guessed I was supposed to go in, so I took a few steps forward, and I heard the door closing behind me.

The room was full of people. They were all working. Some were doing paperwork, others painting the walls, others making clothes... every possible type of work was represented. As I walked down the alleys, no one looked up to see what was happening. They were all working like machines. Eventually I reached the end of the large hall. An old man was sitting on a chair. He looked perfectly normal except for the fact that he was levitating in the air. He was supervising the whole process.

The man looked at me, and his chair started to slowly come down. When the chair touched the ground, he stood up and came towards me.

"Welcome," he said. "It's interesting to see they sent you here as a visitor. You were going to join us soon enough anyway..."

"Who are you?" I asked him. "And who are these people? Why do you keep them here, like prisoners?" If I could have felt anything, I'm sure I would have been angry.

"I am the supervisor of this sector. These people are the souls of the departed. These people are not prisoners. They are here of their own accord."

I was going to ask him why anyone would decide to spend eternity here, but he turned his back on me and started to walk in the direction of a small door at the side of the hall. I decided to follow him.

We walked into a small room. I turned around and saw that the door behind me had disappeared. In front of us were two doors. The one on the right was white, the one on the left was black. They stood out from everything else I had seen here, for the gloominess that accompanied everything was gone. Surprisingly, even the black door had a brightness, or maybe it was an aura of calm.

"Welcome to the room of choice," said the supervisor. "This is where you decide your destiny." I looked at him, he stared back. In his eyes, I saw only one emotion. It took me a few minutes to realise what it was: regret.

He then carried on. "You can choose the white door, and see what happens next. I do not know what awaits you behind this door, nobody who has ever gone through it has ever come back to tell us. You can choose the black door and stay here, and not feel anything. No more sadness, no more fear, no more pain."

"But no more joy or happiness either..." I said in a whisper. I suddenly realised that all those people were here because they had chosen to sacrifice all the good things that life could bring for the sole purpose of not having to experience the bad things ever again. They were probably people like me, people who had refused to see the good and wanted to escape the bad. Once again, two voices rose in my head. The reason I had been standing at the top of the bridge was to escape the pain in my life. But was it worth losing the pain, if it meant losing the joy at the same time?

The old man looked at me and smiled. He knew. He had seen what happened while I made my choice. I had made my decision. I walked towards the white door, looked back at the old man one last time, and opened it.

I was blinded by an intense brightness, of no particular colour. A moment later, I found myself back on top of the bridge, staring at the water.

The soft breeze brushed against my face and the flowing water now sounded like a melody. I climbed over the rail, back to the safe side. I looked down again and smiled. I turned around and took the way that would lead me home. Now I felt fear, but the fear was strangely comforting. My worries of yesterday were still there and were in fact stronger, for the easy option had gone, but I walked on thinking that maybe spending a bit more time on this earth might be worth it after all.

DOMINIC FREESTON is 16 and lives in Whitley Bay in North Tyneside. Dominic grew up in Quebec, Canada and only started writing in English when his family moved to England two years ago. He is interested in "questions about the meaning of life and what comes after" and admires "musicians, scientists and writers and anyone who contributes to make the world a better place, or helps us to see it differently". He admires the work of fellow authors Terry Pratchett and JRR Tolkien. If his musical ambitions don't take off he hopes to study technology and engineering.

Love, sex and cider

Paul Charlton

'Howay mate, we'll give you a quid. Go on, please. Two quid and three fags. Good'ons an'all. Lambert and Butler, none of that Regal crap."

We're stood outside Boozebusters and it's half eight. Connor, that's my mate, is asking everyone who goes past to go in the shop for us. No luck though. I'm sat on the wall next to the shop, watching the clouds. Big grey clouds that are fit to burst. I'm still satched from the last shower half an hour ago and if it starts raining again I'm going home. I don't care what he says. I glance down to see where he's at and notice a big fat woman storming towards me, her flab bouncing along with every step she takes. She points at me like a teacher and opens her big fat gob.

"I know your game son and you won't be getting any alcohol from my shop. Now get away home, isn't it past your bedtime?"

"Piss off," I say, not looking at her. "It's a free country." I'm looking desperately for Connor. I hate it when people come up to me. I get all panicky. My eyes start to water and it looks like I'm going to cry. But I'm not! I'm not soft or anything. It's my adrenalin. The woman's stood there flinging her arms around, trying to scare me off, like I'm some kind of stray dog that's going to crap on her doorstep. I can feel my heart in my belly, beating and beating. But I can't not say anything. So I manage to put my deep voice on, as if I don't care.

"I don't even want drink from your shop. But it's a free country, so I'll sit here till I want to move. So go and call the cops if you want. They won't do owt." Then I stop, because I see that Connor's spotted the woman and is running over.

"Excuse me, excuse me, missus," he shouts, not knowing who she is. "Will you go in the shop for us?"

I start to laugh and it makes me feel a bit better. I'm trying to stop, but I can't. It's like when you're in biology and Mr Bowe talks about fannies. Connor's looking at me wondering why I'm laughing and the big fat woman turns round and grabs hold of him.

"Will I go in the shop for you? Yeah I will, I'll go in there and ring the police you little bastards! I've told your lot before." She's fuming and her face has gone as red as a beetroot. Connor's pointing at her and laughing. I wish I was like him. He doesn't get rattled at all.

"Get off me you stupid cow! Touch me again and I'll call the coppers on you, you big fat beetroot. Look at the state of you." He says this without breathing or blinking or anything. He's class. The woman just stands there, stuttering. Connor copies her and he's mocking her so much she stutters even more.

"Howay lady, spit it out. You w-w-w-w-what. Go and roll back into your shop." Connor's laughing now, but I can tell he hasn't finished with her, he'll take it too far, he always does. So I get off the wall and start moving away from the shop and shout at him to leave it. Luckily he listens to me, which is unusual, and starts walking towards me.

"See you later fatty," he says, pretending to be simple. "Don't get stuck in the doorway when you go back in the shop, will you." We both laugh and walk off, but it's raining again and I'm freezing. I want to go home, but Connor'll just start moaning. The only reason I've come out at all is because Rachael's going to be out. Rachael's gorgeous.

Rachael! Rachael! Rachael!!! I say her name all the time. Sometimes in my head, like when I'm at school and other times I say it out loud, like when I'm in bed. The word sounds class. I don't know what it is. I mean, I know they're just letters put together to make a word. But it's not just a word, it's a feeling. It's like when I made a card for my form tutor in the first year saying thanks for sorting out this lad that bullied us. Her eyes filled up because she wasn't expecting it and I was expecting her not to expect it and that made my eyes start to water, which I didn't expect at all. Then my body got this feeling like warm electricity passing through it. Up to my throat and then my head. It's the best feeling in the world. I can understand why people cry when they're happy, it's the warm electricity that does it every time.

Rachael's got long dark hair and deep brown eyes that bulge out, but in a good way. I always think you could jump in them and bounce up and down like a bouncy castle. Her body's amazing as well. And her tits. Phwaaaar!!! I could get both my hands on one, that's how big they are! She's a 32C. Massive!!! They only go up to 32D, so she's got the second biggest size tits that you can get, except for when you get old and then they look mingin' anyway. She told me the size last week. She tells me all sorts. Even let me look at the tag on her bra when I said I didn't believe her. Then I got a stiffy and I was wearing tracky bottoms and I had to lean forward for ten minutes so she didn't notice. If it was Connor with the stiffy, he'd of just pointed at it and told everyone. That's what he's like. It's probably why Rachael goes out with him and why he gets loads of shags.

Even though he's going out with Rachael, he still meets other lasses. I think it's shocking. He's my mate, so I won't tell Rachael, but she's my mate too, just in a different way. So I feel bad. With Connor I talk about lads stuff, like footy and what birds in our year we want to shag, then with Rachael I can talk about some of my thoughts and feelings. I just don't talk about the feelings I have for her.

She must like me a bit, because she says she wants to marry me when we're twenty five. She goes on about it all the time. Last Friday we were sat in the park as usual, but it was just me and her. Connor had gone to piss on this old woman's door across the road and Jill had gone to watch. This old woman always calls the cops on us, so Connor said she deserved it. Anyway, as soon as they'd gone she slid right up next to me on the roundabout and cuddled into me. I knew what was coming and my heart was in my belly again.

"Egg shell blue!" she blurted out.

"What?"

"The colour of the bridesmaid dresses. Eggshell blue. It'll be lovely." She was smiling at me and I felt class. I was the only person she was looking at. Just me! But at the same time I hated it. She always flirts with me, but she won't go out with me. I look at her and groan as if I don't want to talk about it. I do want to really and she knows that, but I do it anyway.

"We haven't talked about our wedding in ages," she said, laughing.

"Have you set a date yet?" I asked. But I was annoyed with myself. I had five minutes with her to myself and I was asking her stupid questions like that. When all I really wanted to say was, "Why him and not me?" I knew there was no point though. I already knew the answer. So I just played along for those five minutes and by the time they came back I was buzzin'! For a bit anyway. Then I sat and thought about how much I'd have to improve as a person to get her. After that I was just on a total downer. Connor would always be better than me, in every way you could think of.

"So she grabbed my knob and said I had to take her round the back of the youthy and shag her up against the wall," Connor exclaims while we're waiting for someone to go in the shop for us. Every Friday the same thing. We wait in the rain outside the shop and Connor talks about the lasses he's shagged until we eventually find someone to go in for us.

"And you did?" I say, amazed.

"She had hold of me dick! I had to. But it's not being unfaithful. If a lass grabs your dick and says you have to shag her, then you have to shag her. Especially if she's in year ten."

"If you shag someone else you're being unfaithful Connor."

"Listen Jonathan! If you tell her, I'll break your nose. It was the lass that wanted me first, so I was still faithful."

When he called me by my proper name I knew to back off. He was either going to hit me or make me look stupid. He does that quite a bit. So I know the signs. He wants me to ask him about this girl, so that's what I do. I just hope he doesn't start asking me if I shagged Rachael's mate, Jill. He always does that as well. He says when she's pissed I should try. Even though she's a bit mingin'.

"Was she good?" I say, trying to change his mood and distract him.

"No. She laid there like a sack of spuds. Shite man!"

"I thought you shagged her standing up?" As soon as I said it I regretted it. He'd get pissed off and start calling me a virgin again.

"Yeah, but you always have to change positions at least twice. Y'divvy virgin."

Then the typical attack came. Getting quizzed about why I was still a virgin at fourteen when there was only swats and weirdos that were still virgins at my age. Just for once I wanted to shut him up. I wouldn't normally lie, but he was doing my head in. I know he's not a virgin, but he hasn't shagged all the lasses he says he has. And he hasn't shagged Rachael yet. She won't let him, she's got class, not like Jill, she's a slapper. So I said I'd shagged Jill.

"Did you really?" He sounded upset, like I shouldn't have, even though he's always telling me that I should.

"You wouldn't have dared. I'll have bucked fifty lasses before you get a shag." Something in his voice made me think that he kind of believed me, but he wasn't sure.

"I did shag her. Twice!"

"Swear down?"

"Aye."

"Did you wear a blob?"

"Yeah."

"Did it fit?"

"Yeah."

"I don't wear them. They're all too small. I split them."

I was confused. I've never put one on before. I've had hold of one, but never put one on. I was scared to. They looked too big. I thought I must have got an extra large one by accident.

"It, it... I had to squeeze into it," I stutter.

He still wasn't totally sure, so he started telling me about how all the lasses he'd bucked moaned and didn't buck back because he was too big. Unless they were slappers and then the edges of their holes had worn away so they can take more. I just nodded. I didn't have a clue. It worried me a bit as well. I mean, how much of this do I not know and how can I find out properly? It's not as if I can go and ask Mr Bowe in Biology. "Excuse me sir how many times does a lass have to get bucked before she starts to wear away?" I'd get kicked out the class. I hope when I do lose it, it'll be with Rachael, but I can't wait until I'm twenty five. I'll be mocked for years.

I'm lying in bed. I can't move. The pillow is soaking wet with my crying and my mouth's full of salt, like I've swallowed half the ocean. I've been awake for hours and hours now.

My mam's dead. So is my dad. And my sisters. They got malaria and it was too late to help them. They got it after my dad won the money from the *Readers Digest* prize and we went on holiday to Africa.

Just thinking about it cripples me. No one at school knows except Rachael. She's been with me non stop since I told her. She keeps hugging me and kissing me on the cheek and she never lets go of my hand.

"What's the point in living?" I say to her.

"I know it's hard, but it will get better." She hugs me tightly against her chest. I can feel her nipple pressing into me cheek and I start to feel a bit better, but not much.

"I've got no one left. I may as well kill myself, no one would notice anymore."

"That's not true, you've got me. I would notice if you died." She's looking in my eyes and staring really powerfully. The warmth and nice feelings are building up in my stomach.

I sit up and switch my lamp on. My nose is all snotty with my crying and I'm sick of thinking so much. I'm so sad! But not just sad like unhappy, but sad pathetic. I've got a confession to make.

No one died. Not my mam. Not my dad. And not my sisters either. I made it up. I'm a bastard aren't I? I know I am. No one has to tell me, I know I'm sick in the head. I didn't lie to anyone though. I didn't tell anyone this. I just did the whole thing in my head. Pretending in my head that it'd happened and thinking about what Rachael would do to comfort me. That's what I've thought about all night. I feel so horrible! I don't really wish that they were dead, of course I don't! But the whole dream, well sick fantasy really, wasn't about my mam and dad and sisters. It was about Rachael! Just another way of getting her to be with me.

There's something strange and powerful about getting a girl you fancy to feel sorry for you. I don't know what. I wish I didn't think like this. But I do! I think like this all the time. In class I look at her and think about jumping out of the window onto the car park. I could land on my ankles instead of my feet. The drop's quite big. Not scary big, but big enough. Enough for me to break my ankle, but not die or do anything really bad.

Sometimes I think about it that hard that I get a pain in my ankle. Honest! I sit there and go over it in my head. What the fall would be like. What I'd have to do to make a clean break. What the pain would be like. But most of all, what Rachael would do. Hug me. Hold my bag. Help me up steps, and everything. I've considered this in detail for ages. It's divvy really. Here's me, fourteen years old, in my prime, and all I think about is breaking my ankle with a clean break so that Rachael will feel sorry for me. Sometimes I just want to punch myself until I stop being so weird.

I've known that I'm strange for a while. I wasn't always strange. I used to be normal. I am quite normal to look at and to talk to, most of the time. It's just when I start thinking that I get strange. I get lost in my thoughts and they become so real it's scary. I'm too mature. I've definitely got the maturity of a twenty-year-old. Maybe older, like twenty four, or something like that. That's why I'll have loads of girlfriends when I get into the sixth form and the girls stop looking just at older lads and lads that are really good looking. Then they'll start wanting a mature lad. That's when I'll jump in and get so much shagging I'll go dizzy. Not that I want to go dizzy with over-shagging. It'd be nice, but really all I want is Rachael.

It's dark now and I'm waiting on the corner next to the tennis courts for Connor to bring back the cider. I'm even more freezing now, because I've got my coat open so he can put the cider straight down the arms of my big jacket. I look around for the millionth time checking that no one's watching me and everything's clear. I just want to get down the park. My hearts doing the belly thing again and it's worse than with the 'fat woman', because I've got two things to think about. Not just getting caught with the cider, but in five minutes I'll see Rachael. She's in the park with Jill the slapper, waiting for us. I haven't seen her for two and a half days, because she's been off school. So I've got loads to talk to her about.

I'm just thinking about what things I'm going to say and in what order when Connor jumps on my back being a dickhead. It frightens me and I let out a scream like a girl. Connor thinks this is funny and starts laughing his head off. "Shut up man. Someone'll hear us and come outside and if they know my mam I'll get knacked. Howay let's get to the park. Come on." Connor stops laughing just as quickly as he started.

"Don't go shouting at me or I'll bat you. Right?"

Connor jumps the fence to the park and I pass the cider over the top as quickly as I can. My mam's friend's auntie lives a couple of streets away and I'm scared in case she sees me. I do a last check just in case she's watching, then jump over the fence and run to catch Connor up.

When we get across to the swings I get that belly feeling again. Rachael's not here! There's only Jill, she's stood on the roundabout talking to three year ten lasses.

"Hiya," she says. "Rachael can't come cos she's says she's still bad."

"You're joking. It's Friday night!" Connor moans.

"We're going to a party in a bit if you want to come." I'm looking at Jill when she's saying this and I'm thinking that she doesn't really like me. She hasn't looked at me once. She didn't say just for Connor to go to the party, but that's what she meant. It's obvious that she fancies him. Then I get this tingle down my back as a brilliant, but horrible thought comes into my head. What if Connor shags Jill tonight and Rachael finds out? Then she'd split up with Connor and I might have a chance.

"Yeah I'll come, will there be many lasses there?" Connor says.

"About twelve year tens and me," Jill fakely whispers as she smiles at him. That smile says everything. She's had the same idea as me. She wants to shag him! I know it! But they won't if I'm there, so I have to make up an excuse.

"I'm going home I think. I feel bad," I say, almost cringing at my pathetic excuse. But Connor's not bothered. Now that he thinks he'll get a shag at this party, he's not fussed whether I go or not. So I say I'd see him tomorrow and I go off home. I just have to pray that he shags her.

This morning I was up at seven. That's a record for me, I normally sleep until dinner time on a Saturday. Today though, my head's in bits. I'm really hoping that he did shag Jill last night, but at the same time I'm not. It seemed like a brilliant idea last night. Then I went to bed and started thinking about how shockin' it would be if I betrayed my best friend. All just for the smallest chance that Rachael might go out with me. It's like one of those game shows where you have to choose whether to give up the washing machine that you've just won for a chance at winning the jackpot. It's a big decision. A washing machine is a big thing to give up. Like Connor is a big thing. How many other lads that are as sorted as he is, would knock about with me? None, that's how many. So what if I grass on Connor and then Rachael still doesn't want to go out with me? Then I've lost my best mate, upset Rachael, not got a girlfriend and probably I'll get my face smashed in just for good measure. Love's a strange thing.

At half two Connor comes round as usual, so we can listen to the footy on the radio.

"All right Jonny. Did I have a good night last night or what?" His face is beaming and the strut that always looks like he's carrying a dead dog under each arm, now looks like he's carrying The Rock and Hulk Hogan. It's massive. I think his chests going to burst if he pushes it out any further.

"Have you seen Shearer's not playing today?" I mumble.

"Is he not?" Connor says, not really interested. "Listen to this though. You'll never guess what happened at the party last night."

Oh no! He did! He did shag her. I look at him, not saying anything.

"Guess then," he says, waiting impatiently for me to say something. But I can't let on that what he did was what I thought he was going to do. Then he would ask why I was thinking it in the first place.

"How do I know?" I lie. "Rachael came after all?"

"No. But if she did I would have been goosed. If she came she would have caught me bucking Jill. Proper bucking her wild, I was. She bucks back and everything!"

"What about Rachael? Jill's her mate." Yet again my mouth says exactly what my head's thinking. I don't seem to be able to edit my thoughts at all.

"Who are you, like? The buck police or sommat?"

"I was just saying. Will Jill not tell Rachael?"

"No! Of course not. We talked about it afterwards and we've decided to keep it casual. I'm still gonna see Rachael, I'll just buck Jill when I get horny."

I'm listening to him and hating everything about him. How could he be like that? He's trying to sound all grown up saying things like that, but it's just something he's seen on *EastEnders*. I might be a fourteen-year-old virgin that knows nothing about having sex, but at least I don't pretend to be something I'm not. And the way he's talking about Jill is odd. I'm not sure why. Maybe it's because he's never shagged one of Rachael's mates before and he's feeling excited or something. Then I get this thought and it disturbs me a bit. All the way through the first half of the football I'm thinking about it. I don't listen to a word the commentator says, or the crap Connor is talking. I just keep thinking.

What if Connor was a virgin until last night? I know it sounds strange, but there's a chance. The way he's so excited is weird. If he was, then I'm totally confused. Do people really say what they mean? What do you believe and what do you just forget about? And most importantly how many people in my class are still virgins, but just pretend that they're not? I always thought because I'm so mature, I could spot when someone was lying. Pretending to be something that they're not. What if I can't spot it? How do I go to school and believe a word anyone says? When will they lie and for what reason?

Does Rachael lie? If she does, what does she lie about?

I start to hear Connor jabbering on again. He's saying something about smelling his fingers, but I'm not listening. He's disgusting. He deserves to be finished by Rachael. I really think I'm starting to hate him. But do I tell Rachael? What will she do? Then I get another thought and I feel all warm. What if Rachael's lying about wanting to marry me when we're twenty five? What if she really means she wants to marry me now, or at least go out with me, but she's too shy to ask? People always lie for a reason and that's a really good reason.

I've got to get rid of Connor and go and see Rachael. I have to do it now. I'm feeling like I can conquer anything, so it has to be now.

"Arggh," I shout. Making Connor jump.

"What's the matter?" he panics.

"My belly. I've got the pains again. I had them all last night. I think I've ruptured my spleen."

As soon as I say this he gets up and goes home. I know he's squeamish, he hates anything like that. He says he'll come and see me tomorrow. By then he won't be feeling sorry for me, he'll want to kill me. As the front door shuts I jump up and get changed. If I'm going to get Rachael I'll have to look good.

I'm sitting on Rachael's bed with my arms folded tightly, while she messes about with her hair. I daren't unfold my arms, I'm so nervous I've got sweat patches that look like ponds, under my arms. This is the biggest moment of my life!

"Rachael I need to tell you something." I can feel more sweat running from my armpit.

"What?" she says, still playing with her hair.

"It's about sex."

"Sex?" Now I have her attention.

"Yeah, sex. And Connor."

"Jonny!" she giggles. "That's a bit personal. You know I'm not having sex until marriage, so you've got nothing to worry about."

"No, it's not... I mean Connor having sex with someone else."

"You better be joking Jonny." I can see she's going to cry. I shake my head.

"Who was it?" she whimpers.

"Jill," I croak. As soon as I say it she starts screaming. I've never seen her like this before. I feel horrible. I go up to cuddle her, but she pushes me away. I don't know what to say and I can't just ask her out now while she's crying and in such a state.

"You're better off without him. It's his own fault that he's been finished." Again my mouth lets me down. I shouldn't have said all that, so now she's looking at me weirdly.

"I hate him. But I hate her more. She's supposed to be my best friend. It's all her fault."

I could sense that something with my plan had gone wrong. It was like in those movies where the girl forgives the fella no matter what and you end up shouting at the screen telling her to finish him. That's what was going to happen here.

"I won't finish him. I won't give that bitch the satisfaction."

"But you have to, he was unfaithful."

"But he didn't mean it. I still hate him, but I know he won't have meant it."

What do you say to that? You can't say anything. Girls are stupid. The only thing I had left was to ask her out. I'd planned to work up to it slowly, but everything was moving so fast.

"Rachael? Do you hate me?"

"No."

"Do you like me more than Connor?"

"Of course I do." I know she doesn't understand what I'm trying to say.

"W-well if you like me more, why don't you finish him and go out with... with me?" I suddenly realise how stupid I am. She just looks at me. Not a nice look, but a look that says she's just been told that make-up's been banned for life. The tears in her eyes are starting to leak out and I'm sure there's going to be enough to fill a bath.

"Go away Jonny. I can't deal with you right now."

Go away! What does that mean? It isn't a no, but it isn't a yes either. I have to say one last thing and hope that my mouth gets it right.

"I'd be faithful and I'd look after you." There's a whining sound in my voice and I hate it. I sound pathetic. I've said a stupid corny line, something that's in every crappy romantic movie in the world.

"I'm Connor's girlfriend and he might be a bastard, but I'm still his girlfriend."

"But he'll keep shagging Jill." That was my last attack. I have nothing else.

"He wouldn't dare!"

"But why him and not me?"

"Because he's Connor."

That little sentence is like a punch from Lennox Lewis. I've asked for it and it's knocked me on my arse. The one thing that I know and I hate, had just been said. Why would she want me, when she's got him? I start to walk out, but as I get up, my mouth starts to open by itself.

"Well, what does that make me?" I ask.

"Jonny!"

PAUL CHARLTON is 20 and comes from Bishop Auckland. He is currently studying at the Royal Scottish Academy of Music and Drama. He started to write plays when he was 14 and was commissioned by Paines Plough theatre company to write a play when he was 16 as part of Black and White Shorts at Newcastle's Live Theatre. He is inspired by writers such as Lee Hall, John Godber, Tony Parsons and Nick Hornby. He aspires to write work which "you don't need a degree in English Lit to understand".

Bumblebee

I'm a bee so please let me sting you
I will die a lonely death, wrap me up in your tin foil
The dirt under my fingernails is clean, it is mine
But I don't like your world, because your world is soiled

Scared, alone, crippled, susceptible
Silver stars that shimmer, and in their iridescence
I see myself, and maybe what I really am
I'm just a bumblebee, learning life's lessons

Ellie Slee

ELLIE SLEE is 13 and lives in County Durham. She began writing when she was four. Her poem is inspired by her sister "bringing bees home and wrapping them up in tin foil. Bumble bees are so pretty it's sad that they die so quickly". Ellie plays bass guitar, plays her music very loud and "worries her mother to death". When she is older she would love to be "something glamorous", like a fashion designer or fashion journalist.

Memory Woman

She says she's like a memory woman
Who's far too old to be worrying about
Standing on the cracks,
But however hard she shuts her eyes
The memories came creeping back.

She says she's like a memory woman
With floss and fur and smell of cat
And the dust in a sunlight beam
And a collar and a word,
The smell of someone's perfume
On a breeze that blew away summer too soon.

She said, as the dark nights came riding,
That now it was winter and memories itching
Like cinders, she would have to throw herself
Like a bird with a broken wing from the nest,
Just hope for the best, she laughed and she laughed.
And then she cried.

She said she was a million fingers and a million toes
All touching in darkness, and a million memories
Moving her in and out of time.
She said her voice was cut like glass
And her eyes were sirens for what she'd seen
And that the moths in her clothes had been there for ages,
They just fluttered when flight took their fancy
To move like dust.

Clapped her hands and saw the sun,
Saw the winter sky sharp and edgy,
Saw a bird hover and the traffic light change
When there was nobody there,
Watched a leaf fall an ant crawl and a
Woman slapping her son.

She saw a man cross the road
With a walking stick,

Tasted Christmas in a gulp of air
And remembered that once,
When she saw the moon rise orange
Over a mountain and she travelled
Fast in a car with the wind in her hair
That once there was the taste of wine and laughter
And the shadow of herself dancing upon the wall.

Emma McGordon

Heat

Sex on the red covers,
The blue, the white, the green.
His breath, her mouth, all of it
Without ever letting go of her hand.
Far flung fighter blade
Faster touches the feather into surrender.
Heat, heat,
Heat on heart like a mantle.
The triple touch,
The smile,
In a while, it'll be morning.
She'll be alone;
Burned out star;
Empty shell;
Waveless ocean
Calm as stone

Emma McGordon

When Hitler was my Daddy

When Hitler was my daddy, we'd march for miles
In our gleaming green emerald German fields, saluting the

Stars, which always held an extra twinkle when Daddy's eye
Was upon them. I, with stuffupperlip and index finger perfectly poised,

Pretended that I too had a brilliant, resilient to Shaving moustache like
Daddy's and a fabulous Fuhrer grin that smirked at words like gas.

Sometimes, on my knees, I'd spit spit spit on Daddy's pure German
Leather knee boots and shine them to a starry spangled banner shine,

On the German germ-free soil. He'd tie me to the big tree, scratching
My spine on the bark like a bald coyote I'd howl in the dark

At the silver moon spreading its pearly plan that crept like a bad
Shadow over Daddy's German standing upright grass.

On the last walk with Daddy, (oh how he was smiling) I turned
To count one-two-million Jew on my newly bought by Daddy abacus

When the bullet rang. With speed of startled child I turned to see,
Gun still at his head, Darling Daddy Hitler lying Darling Daddy Dead.

Emma McGordon

EMMA McGORDON is 19 and lives in Whitehaven in Cumbria. She has been writing since she was five and writing seriously since she was 13. She is inspired by other poets and by the songs of Bob Dylan. She aims to "write as much as possible, live my life and see what's around the next corner".

What is New Writing North?

New Writing North is the writing development agency for the Northern Arts area (Teesside, Wearside, County Durham and Northumberland). The organisation was created in 1996 to support writers who lived and worked in the region and to offer advice and encouragement to aspiring writers.

Writers are supported by a range of awards and bursaries operated by NWN, most notably the Northern Writers' Awards (worth up to £22,000 a year) and the Northern Rock Foundation Writer's Award (£60,000 to the winning writer). Aspiring writers also receive support via mentoring and career development initiatives and training.

New Writing North also produces live literature events, writers' residencies, literature development projects and theatre writing projects and runs a number of career development courses for writers. The company recently appointed an education director who oversees all of our work which involves schools and young people.

We are also developing an international element to our work with series of projects which will see us working with writers from around the world.

Our previous work includes: writers in residence with Nexus, the Post Office, The Great North Run, Newcastle Education Action Zone, Ashington Education Action Zone and Hartlepool Museums; festival programmes for Durham Literature Festival and Sunderland Arts and Libraries; theatre development projects with Live Theatre, Northern Stage and NTC Theatre and media projects with BBC Radio, Yorkshire Television and Northern Film and Media.

Some current projects: 2003-2004

KOOCH CINEMA	Creative writing and filmmaking project with Iranian refugees and asylum seekers
DRAMA COMMISSIONS	Experimental commissions for new performance work
LINGUA FRANCA	Live literature and international events programme
FILM PROJECTS	Short film projects with schools in Easington and Darlington
WEST PARK	Large-scale creative writing project in Darlington with schools and property developers Bussey and Armstrong
WRITERS IN SCHOOLS	A range of writing residencies in Newcastle, County Durham, Hartlepool and Sunderland schools
WRITE ON TYNE	Writer in residence with BBC Tyne website: www.bbc.co.uk/tyne
WRITERS' CENTRE	Development of a centre for creative writing in collaboration with Newcastle University
IGNITE RADIO COURSE	Course for writers to learn more about writing for radio, in conjunction with Sunderland University
COURSES FOR WRITERS	Career development courses for writers across the region

Want to learn more?

For more information about New Writing North's work and for up to date literary and theatre news please see our website:

www.newwritingnorth.com

The site also features free downloads of writing guides written by professional writes from the north east.

New Writing North
7-8 Trinity Chare
Quayside,
Newcastle upon Tyne
NE1 3DF
T: 0191 232 9991
E: mail@newwritingnorth.com

Director: Claire Malcolm
Education Director: Anna Summerford
Finance and Administration Manager: Silvana Michelini

Patrons: Pat Barker, Sean O'Brien and Peter Flannery

Registered Charity no: 1062729
Company limited by guarantee: 3166037

Board members: Lesley Aers, Andy Croft, John Dodds, Chrissie Glazebrook, Tony Harrington, WN Herbert, Pauline Moger (chair), Caroline Redmond (vice chair), Wils Wilson, Wendy Robertson, Annie Wright

New Writing North is managed by a voluntary board of trustees. We would like to take this opportunity to thank them for their dedication and hard work.